QUEEN SOPHIE HARTLEY

Stephanie Greene

All rights reserved. Published in the United States by Sandpiper, an imprint of Houghton Mifflin
Harcourt Publishing Company. Originally published in hardcover in the United States by
Clarion Books, an imprint of Houghton Mifflin Harcourt Publishing Company, 2005.

SANDPIPER and the SANDPIPER logo are trademarks of
Houghton Mifflin Harcourt Publishing Company.

For information about permission to reproduce selections from this book,
write to Permissions, Houghton Mifflin Harcourt Publishing Company,
215 Park Avenue South, New York, New York 10003.

www.hmhbooks.com

The text of this book is set in 14-point Giovanni Book.

The Library of Congress has cataloged the hardcover edition as follows:
Greene, Stephanie.
Queen Sophie Hartley / by Stephanie Greene.
p. cm.
Summary: A suggestion from her mother leads Sophie to befriend the new girl at school and
an elderly, grouchy woman, and helps her overcome the feeling that she is not good at anything.
[1. Self-confidence—Fiction. 2. Family life—Ohio—Fiction. 3. Friendship—Fiction.
4. Old age—Fiction. 5. Schools—Fiction. 6. Ohio—Fiction] I. Title.
PZ7.G8434Qu 2005
[Fic]—dc22   2004020106

ISBN: 978-0-618-49461-3 hardcover
ISBN: 978-0-547-55021-3 paperback

Manufactured in the United States of America
DOM 10 9 8 7 6 5 4 3 2 1

4500297044

For Dinah, with thanks

Chapter One

The day Nora and Sophie's ballet teacher, Mrs. Ogilvy, told their mother after the recital that Nora should continue her lessons, but "I wouldn't waste any more money on Sophie," was not a good day in the Hartley household.

First, because Sophie and Nora heard. And second, because when Mrs. Hartley told their father about it in the living room before dinner as the girls were going up the stairs, Mr. Hartley said, "What did I tell you?"

The girls heard that, too.

Sophie ran upstairs and flung herself on her twin bed in the room she shared with Nora and sobbed for a few minutes. They were deep, heartfelt sobs, and as she sobbed, a tiny part of her listened. It was really very satisfying to think how wronged and sad she sounded. But it was a bit of a waste, too, because nobody came up to check on her for what felt like a very long time, so when Nora was finally finished in the bathroom and came into their room carrying her ballet bag, Sophie was feeling much better. Crying cheered her up, but she didn't want Nora to know that. Sympathy cheered her up even more.

"Even Daddy thinks I'm fat and clumsy," she said to her older sister in as pitiful a voice as she could muster.

"He didn't say anything about your weight," Nora said. She didn't cast so much as a sympathetic look in Sophie's direction as she opened their closet door and slipped her pink ballet slippers neatly into the two slots reserved for them in her shoe bag.

"It's your own fault, anyway," she went on after she had shut the door and turned back around. "Mrs. Ogilvy told you not to wear those shoes, and you did."

"I *like* them," said Sophie. She gave a self-righteous little sniff, but she knew Nora was right. Mrs. Ogilvy had told the beginners' class they were to wear their ballet slippers, tights, and white leotards for the recital, but Sophie hadn't been able to resist wearing her new shoes. She adored them. They were the most beautiful things she had ever owned.

They were pink velvet covered with red roses. Embroidered roses with bright red petals and delicate green stems. Best of all, each rose had a tiny diamond in the middle. Well, maybe they weren't *real* diamonds, but they looked like real diamonds. They sparkled like real diamonds, too. They would go perfectly with the diamond tiara Sophie was saving up for. She had been cutting pictures of people wearing tiaras out of the newspaper and magazines for months. She kept them in the drawer of her bedside table. There were pictures of real queens wearing tiaras, actresses in movies wearing tiaras, and the past two Miss Americas in their tiaras.

She even had a picture of a dog wearing one.

Sometimes Sophie put a book on her head and practiced walking slowly around her room with her chin up and her head very still, the way she imagined she would have to walk when she finally got her tiara. She was planning on wearing it all day, every day, for as long as she lived. Everyone would have to curtsy to her.

Even Nora.

Until then, her pink velvet shoes would have to do. They were wonderful. Even the straps were special. They could be worn up or down.

Which is where Sophie got into trouble.

She was supposed to wear her shoes with the straps up because they were too big. Her mother had bought them that way on purpose. Mrs. Hartley always bought their party shoes a size too big so that Nora and Sophie wouldn't outgrow them before they could wear them out. She told Sophie to wear them with the straps up to keep them on until her feet got bigger.

But Sophie didn't like wearing them with the straps up. They felt like little-girl shoes.

With the straps down, it was a different story. Sophie thought they looked sophisticated with the straps down. She didn't care if they *did* slip off her heels with every step she took.

"You were supposed to be a *snowflake*, for heaven's sake, and *drift* across the stage," Nora said. "That's what the rest of your class did. But not you! You clopped all over the stage the entire recital. You sounded more like a hailstorm! Everyone could hear you. I was so embarrassed, I almost died."

"*I* wasn't embarrassed," said Sophie. She wanted to say, I felt beautiful, but she knew it would make Nora mad.

"Well, you should have been." Nora shoved her leotard into her top drawer without folding it and slammed the drawer shut, which meant she was already mad. After a life of sharing a bedroom with her sister, Sophie knew that Nora usually took very good care of her clothing. She folded everything neatly and even buttoned all the buttons on her sweaters before she put them away. When she started stuffing things into her drawers, it was a bad sign.

Sophie tried one last sniff, in case Nora had a thread of sympathy in her, but it was no good. Her nose was dry.

"You hate ballet, Sophie, you know you do," Nora said in a reasonable, annoying-older-sister kind of way. "You only took it because you were giving us all headaches with the violin. And the only reason you took the violin was because Thad takes it."

"I liked the smell of the rosin," said Sophie.

"And look what happened with your riding lessons," Nora went on. "You only wanted to ride horses because the girl in that book you were reading rode horses. You *hated* it."

"It made my bottom sore."

"I don't know how it could have." Nora picked up her hairbrush, gave a quick glance at the rounded half moon of Sophie's belly peeking out between the top of her shorts and the bottom of her shirt, and bent over to brush her hair one hundred strokes. "You have enough padding," she said from behind a curtain of hair.

Sophie tugged half-heartedly at her shirt.

She knew how much her stomach annoyed Nora. Nora was always showing her how she should take a deep breath and suck in her stomach and then throw her shoulders back so she would look better. But when she did all of that, Sophie could hardly walk, much less breathe. And she didn't understand why a flat stomach was so wonderful in the first place. She was certainly never going to stand sideways in front of the full-length mirror on their closet door and smooth her shirt down over her stomach every night to check on it, the way Nora did. Or watch every little thing she put into her mouth and jump on and off the scale all the time like it was a trampoline.

"And now look what you've done," said Nora. She had stood up suddenly and sent a great wave of dark hair flying back over her head. "You've made a mess of your bedspread again. Before you know it, you'll be crying about *that*."

Sophie looked. There was a large damp spot on her spread right under the edge of her pillow. She wiped at it with the sleeve of her shirt. "Crying makes me feel better," she said.

"It wouldn't if you knew how disgusting you look," Nora said. "Most people look horrible when they cry. Eyes rimmed with red, like horrible possums, noses dripping." She shuddered. "I never cry, it makes such a mess."

Nora had been telling Sophie she looked disgusting for as long as she could remember; Sophie was used to it. She admired her older sister enormously even so. She could have been jealous of Nora, but she wasn't. There were too many nights when Nora had let Sophie crawl into bed with her and huddle under the blanket during thunderstorms. And all the times Nora had walked on the outside to protect her when they passed the brick house on the corner because Sophie had been afraid of the huge black lab that lived there.

Besides, back when they were younger, Nora used to come up with the most wonderful plays. Nora assigned the parts, of course, and always got to be the princess because she was the oldest and the prettiest, as she told Sophie. But Sophie didn't mind. The princess never seemed to *do* anything except sit in front of the mirror and comb her hair. Sophie had much more fun being the frog and hopping all over. Or sticking a wad of old gum on the end of her nose and mixing everything she could find in the kitchen cabinets in a big pot when she was the ugly witch.

Still, it was hard, sometimes, having a perfect sister. Even at twelve, Nora looked like the prima ballerina she said she was going to be when she grew up. Sophie didn't doubt it for a minute. And lately, things between them had changed. Sophie wasn't afraid of dogs anymore; now she fell in love with every mangy dog she saw and longed to drag it home. And ever since Nora had started marking off on the calendar the months until she turned thirteen, Sophie wouldn't have *dared* ask to jump into her bed even if the whole house was under water and it was the only thing still afloat.

These days, Nora didn't even want Sophie to step on her side of the room. She had actually made a line on the rug between their beds with masking tape. Sophie wasn't supposed to cross it. For a few days, Sophie had gamely tried jumping from the doorway to her bed without touching the floor, but when she fell short one night and almost got a concussion on her bedpost, their mother made Nora take the tape up.

Sophie sighed. She didn't know what had changed, but Nora acted as if she was angry with Sophie half the time. Being around Nora was like walking on eggshells. Sophie didn't think *she* was the one who had changed. But she was careful just the same.

"Why don't you do something *you're* good at instead of always doing things the rest of us are good at?" said Nora.

"Because I'm not good at anything."

The minute she said it, Sophie remembered her list. She had been working on it for weeks. Now she had one more thing to add to it, she thought with satisfaction.

Sophie hadn't told Nora about her list. She hadn't told anyone. A list of things she was bad at was not something she wanted to have fall into anyone else's hands. Especially not in her family, where everyone else was good at something. In addition to playing the violin, her older brother, Thad, was co-captain of the soccer team. Nora was such a good dancer she was auditioning for the lead in the spring performance their ballet school was putting on. Even John—who at six was almost three years younger than Sophie—could draw funny cartoons. It didn't seem to matter that his characters were always either blowing things up or hanging from cliffs, and that there was at least one knife with blood dripping from its point in every picture. They made people laugh.

As for Maura . . . Sophie sighed. Maura was good at being a baby, she thought resignedly. That's the only thing babies *had* to be good at to get all the attention. Sophie might have started feeling sorry for herself again if it hadn't been for her list. She had hidden it in a spot where no one would find it. She wanted to get it out now and add ballet.

"You're good at crying—that's something," said Nora. She had stopped brushing her hair and was smoothing it away from her forehead with a hair band. Her dark hair was almost as curly as Sophie's, but Nora wouldn't allow it to curl. She dried it with a dryer every night and sprayed things on it and spent a great deal of time trying to tame it until not a hair was out of place. Like now.

"You *should* be good at it," Nora added. "You do it enough."

It was obvious she was bored with the whole subject. Sophie was bored with it, too, because what Nora said had given her a sudden, wonderful idea. All she wanted was for Nora to leave so she could take out her list.

"Well, you're not very good at making me feel better," said Sophie.

"I don't have to be. You've already stopped crying. You turn it on and off like a faucet, Sophie. You know you do."

"Oh, go away and leave me alone," Sophie said ungratefully. She threw herself down on her bed to make it look as if she was about to start crying again.

"Fine with me," said Nora. "There's far too

much navel contemplation going on in this room for my taste."

The minute she left, Sophie sat up; thinking about her list made her feel remarkably cheerful. As for the navel contemplation, that was what their mother always warned them about. It didn't mean they couldn't look at their belly buttons if they wanted to. Mr. and Mrs. Hartley laughed when they did that. In fact, back before Maura was born and Thad and Nora got too old and thought it was silly, they used to line up in a row and compare belly buttons from time to time. Thad and Sophie had "outies," John had an "innie," and Nora had what looked like a perfect circle divided into two equal halves.

There was still a photograph on the refrigerator door of the four of them standing side by side, holding up their T-shirts and grinning.

Navel contemplation was something different, Sophie knew. According to Mrs. Hartley, it meant thinking about yourself too much. Focusing on your own worries and problems.

She told her children that contemplating their navels would only make them feel sorry for themselves and that there were too many people going around feeling sorry for themselves as it was. The world would be a far better place if people went around feeling sorry for *other* people for a change, she said.

They were all used to their mother talking this way. Mrs. Hartley was a nurse. Before the children were born, she had worked in a hospital. Now she worked part-time taking care of people in their own houses. She saw so many people who were truly in bad shape that she was forever lecturing her children about the need for them to "get on with it," as she put it.

That was fine for Nora and Thad, Sophie thought as she opened the top drawer of her dresser. They both had things they could get on with.

She felt around at the back of her underwear drawer. It was filled with clean underpants and dirty socks. Her mother would be horrified if she saw them. She never did see them, though, because while it was her job to wash the family's clothes, it was each person's job to put them away. Mrs. Hartley left the clothes in neat little piles in the laundry room under signs with their names. Half the time, Thad and John changed right there.

Sophie, however, liked to put her own things away. That way, her mother never saw what was going on. She never knew, for instance, that Sophie wore her socks for a week at a time before putting them in the hamper. Sophie liked her socks dirty. She liked the way they held the shape of her foot so that it looked as if her feet were still in them. She liked the way they got softer and softer the more times she wore them, too. Even the smell didn't bother her.

Sophie felt the familiar crinkle of paper and pulled out her blue socks with the yellow butterflies. She sat down on her bed, took out the piece of paper she'd stuffed into the ball, and smoothed it over her knees. Then she looked at it and sighed. The list of her weaknesses seemed to be getting longer and longer.

Things I Am Bad At:
   Tooth brushing
   Cursive
   Sitting still
   Violin
   Horseback riding
   Gymnastics
   Hair brushing

Sophie was nothing if not truthful, so she picked up a pencil and carefully added "Ballet" to the bottom. Then she turned the paper over and wrote another heading, because the wonderful idea that had come to her while she was talking to Nora was that she would start a second list.

This list would be things she was good at.

Things I Am Good At, Sophie wrote carefully. She immediately wrote "Crying" at the top and then looked at it and frowned. Did one thing make a list? she wondered. She thought not, and chewed furiously on the end of her pencil for a few minutes while she racked her brain for something else she could add.

And then it came to her.

"Stopping crying" she wrote triumphantly. There. That looked much better. Sophie stuffed her list back into her sock and jumped up off her bed. She was glad the job was done, because so much thinking had made her hungry. Judging from the smell of onions wafting up the stairs, they were having hamburgers smothered with fried onions for dinner. Thank heavens it wasn't liver, Sophie thought; they were due for liver any night now. She knew because she kept track. Mrs. Hartley insisted they have liver on a regular basis because it was so good for them. But they all hated it.

At least tonight was going to be delicious, she thought cheerfully. Since she wasn't going to be a ballerina anymore, it didn't matter how much she ate, did it? And Nora was wrong about tears, she decided as she looked at herself in the mirror. They weren't horrible, they were interesting. Hers had left dirty tracks down her cheeks that her mother was sure to notice. Maybe she would be extra nice to Sophie at dinner.

With a tremendous sigh of satisfaction, Sophie stuffed her socks back in her drawer. Making lists was another thing she was good at. No other member of the family was as good at it as she was. In fact, there wasn't another list in any other underwear drawer in the house.

Sophie knew, because she'd looked.

Any list that wasn't worth hiding in your underwear drawer wasn't worth reading, she told herself firmly. She went down to dinner a happy girl.

Chapter Two

But after a quick glance at Sophie's upturned face, all Mrs. Hartley said to her was, "And wash your face before you sit down." She was busy putting steaming food into bowls and had barely looked around when Sophie came up to her. Sophie went into the bathroom, picked up the damp towel someone had left in a wad on the sink, and quickly ran it over her mouth. Then she took her place at the table. She didn't bother to sulk because she knew it wouldn't do any good. No one in her family paid any attention to heavy silences and dark looks.

Especially not at dinner. They were all too

busy spinning the lazy Susan in the middle of the kitchen table around and around, grabbing food. Sophie took a hamburger and carefully piled on a generous amount of onions, ketchup, relish, and mustard. The minute she took her first bite, a good-sized glop of it fell out onto her lap. She quickly scooped it up with her finger and put it in her mouth before anyone could notice.

Thad was telling their father about the goal he'd scored in a soccer game that afternoon. He kept jumping out of his chair and making lunging moves to show Mr. Hartley exactly how he'd saved the day. Every time he hopped up, Mrs. Hartley told him automatically to sit down. Then she'd get involved trying to keep Maura from smearing more squash all over her face and Thad would hop up again.

All the action made it possible for Sophie to sneak another handful of French fries without her mother noticing. When her belly felt as if it was about to explode, though, and she had to unbutton the top button on her shorts to make room for dessert, she started feeling sorry for herself again. She was glad her mother hadn't nagged her, but it would have been nice if she'd showed a *tiny* bit of sympathy, knowing how cruel Mrs. Ogilvy had been to her that afternoon.

As usual, though, Mrs. Hartley was occupied with Maura.

Not for the first time, Sophie wished her mother would stop paying so much attention to Maura and pay attention to her. It wasn't that Sophie didn't love Maura—she did. She loved to play with her and watch her while she took her bath. She especially loved to be the first one into Maura's room when she woke up from her nap; Maura always looked so grateful. Sophie knew Maura was glad to see *anyone* who was going to lift her out of the prison of her crib, but deep inside she couldn't help but think that Maura was just a little happier to see *her.*

Mrs. Hartley said she loved all her children the same, and Sophie believed her. But she certainly seemed to spend a lot more time fussing over Maura than she did over any of the others. Sophie couldn't remember the last time her mother had wiped *her* chin, she thought grumpily as she watched her mother first wipe Maura's face and then kiss it. She would have hated it, of course, but still.

All her mother ever did was say, "Sophie, you look a mess. Go wash your face." And not very nicely, either. Thinking about how unfairly she was treated, Sophie sighed heavily, and her mother gave her a sharp look.

"What, did you eat too much again?" she asked. Sophie didn't think her mother sounded at all sympathetic, so she didn't answer.

"She had two helpings of French fries," Nora piped up.

"Nora, don't tattle," Mrs. Hartley said automatically.

"I can eat all I want now that I'm not taking ballet," Sophie said to Nora. She crammed two more French fries into her mouth and chewed with her mouth open, knowing it would gross her out. But Nora wasn't watching.

"Speaking of ballet," Nora said to their mother quickly, "if Sophie's not going to be taking it, we're going to have much more money. Can I have new ballet slippers? Mine have a hole in them."

The Hartley children were all very aware of money. Mrs. Hartley worked part-time, and Mr. Hartley, who worked for a moving company, said that the furniture he had to carry was a lot heftier than his salary. And when you had five children, Mr. Hartley said, one of them always wanted something. "If I threw a peanut in the middle of the floor, you'd all kill one another trying to get it" is how he put it.

"What's that?" said Thad, looking at his sisters with sudden interest. "Sophie bombed out again?"

"Mrs. Ogilvy said her lessons were a waste of money," said Nora.

"Way to go, Soph!" said Thad. He rose halfway out of his seat and leaned across the table to give her a friendly punch on the shoulder.

It didn't really hurt, and she knew he was only teasing, but Sophie said "Ouch" anyway and rubbed her arm, hoping her mother would yell at him for being mean.

She didn't. She just said, "Sit down, Thad," again and went on taking care of Maura.

"I need some torpedoes," John said suddenly. They all turned to look at him. He was sitting at one end of the table, next to his father. Even with the phone book on his chair, his chin barely cleared the top of the table. "And some tanks and some bombs," he added.

"So you're the one who's been adding things to my grocery list," said Mrs. Hartley. "Only it said 'b-o-m-s.' I didn't know what that meant."

"Sophie spelled it for me," said John.

"Sophie, really," Mrs. Hartley said irritably. "It's bombs! There's a silent *b*! B-o-m-b-s! You should be a better speller at your age."

"Does anyone else find this conversation as strange as I do?" said Nora to no one in particular. "My six-year-old brother wants bombs and torpedoes, and all my mother cares about is spelling."

"And tanks," John said to her.

"Yes, really, Sophie," Mrs. Hartley said, as if

John's recent military mania was all Sophie's fault. "I asked you not to encourage him."

"He doesn't want to *do* anything with them," said Sophie.

A few weeks earlier at dinner, John had announced he wanted to join the army. It had created quite a stir. Sophie hadn't understood what all the fuss was about.

"You don't want to be in the army, John," Mrs. Hartley had said to him in the reasonable voice she used when she was confident that simple logic would change one of her children's minds. "You'd have to *shoot* people."

"Not people," John said. "The enemy."

"But the enemy *is* people," said his mother.

John had just given her a dark look that meant she didn't understand and hunched his shoulders. "I want to for the boots," he said.

Sophie understood immediately. As soon as they went upstairs after dinner, she fished her old rubber boots out of her closet and took them into John's room, where he was getting ready for bed.

"Here," she said, holding them out. "You can have these."

"Army boots are black," he protested as she forced them on over the slipper feet of his pajamas.

"You have to pretend," Sophie told him firmly. "You make believe they're black until you get the real ones."

John had worn them ever since. To school, to bed. He even wore them in the bathtub one night until Mrs. Hartley discovered him and pulled them off, dumping water all over the bathroom floor. Even when Thad said, "Nice ducks, John," it didn't discourage him.

It was exactly the way Sophie was going to be when she got her tiara. She was very proud of him.

John was wearing his boots now. Bright yellow with red ducks.

"B-o-m-s," her mother said again, shaking her head. "Really, Sophie."

"I only write letters I can hear," Sophie said.

"Good Lord," said her mother, throwing her hands in the air.

"Your report card should be a real hoot," said Nora, after which Thad snapped his fingers and said, "Darn! There goes the spelling bee championship."

Mr. Hartley had been sitting calmly at the head of the table with his after-dinner toothpick sticking out of one side of his mouth, listening. Now he took the toothpick out and said, "Don't you worry about Sophie. One of these days she'll find out what she's all about. Then there'll be no stopping her. Right, Sophie?"

He leaned toward her with both elbows on the table and his sleeves rolled up showing his strong arms, and winked. Sophie sat up a little taller.

It was the first thing he had said the whole meal. She knew it was only because his plate was empty and he wanted them all to stop talking and get to the dessert, but Sophie smiled back at him gratefully. Her father didn't single her out very often, and certainly not to say something complimentary. He was a man of few words, as their mother always said. To which Mr. Hartley always replied, "It's a good thing, too, the way people in this family carry on."

"Well, she'd better find out pretty soon," Nora said ungraciously. "She can't do *anything* right now."

Sophie felt a sudden rush of confidence, thinking about no one being able to stop her. And she was suddenly sick and tired of Nora acting so superior all the time. There *was* one thing she could do that no one else in the family could. She was going to do it now, even though it usually ended badly.

"What about this?" she said brashly. "None of you can do this." Sophie wiggled the muscles in the tip of her nose and felt her nostrils move in and out.

Thad and Mr. Hartley could bend their thumbs back to touch their wrists, and John could fold his eyelids up so that the pale insides showed. But no one else in the family could flare their nostrils.

Mrs. Hartley said, "Oh, Sophie," in an impatient voice, but everyone else started to laugh. It was very nice being the center of attention for a change, so Sophie did it some more. Thad and John started shouting "Olé!" as though she were a bull pawing the ground and blowing hot air out of its huge nose. Her father laughed and said, "She didn't get it from *my* side of the family."

Even Maura clapped her hands because everyone else was having such a good time.

But when Nora put her fingers on her own thin nose and said, "I'd die if *my* nose looked like that," Sophie started to feel a little less pleased. And when Thad held out his napkin as if it was a cape for the bull to charge, her whole mood changed. It suddenly felt as if they weren't laughing *with* her, they were laughing *at* her.

Before she knew it, she was crying.

"You're making fun of me," she wailed, pushing back her chair.

She ran up the stairs and into her room, slamming the door behind her. They were mean, she thought as she flung herself on her bed. She made loud sobbing noises for a bit, and tried to make the tears flow while waiting to hear the footsteps of someone coming up the stairs to console her. No one did, though, and her sobs were starting to sound just the tiniest bit forced, so she stopped. Two times in one day had dried her up inside.

It was really very insulting, she thought as she sat up. The sounds of life were going on downstairs as usual. She heard chairs being pushed back and dishes clinking together as they were stacked. Then the phone ringing and Nora's voice. When she finally heard the television spring into life and realized that her father was sitting in front of it with Maura on his lap, Sophie gave up.

Here she'd had her heart nearly broken, and nobody even cared.

She went and stood in front of the mirror. In all the times she had flared her nostrils to get attention and then ended up running up to her room, no one *ever* came to see how she was, she thought tragically. It would serve them right if she stopped doing it. She creased her forehead and bent her mouth into several different shapes to see how sad she could look, but she soon got tired of it. Being upset wasn't very satisfying if nobody was around to feel sorry for you.

Sophie pressed her lips together and puffed out her cheeks as far as they would go, then tried to flare her nostrils again. They didn't flare nearly as much that way, she always noticed. She let out a little puff of air to deflate her cheeks and tried again. Her nose *did* rather look like a bull's, but it was mean of Thad to say so.

The sound of footsteps coming down the hall caught her off guard. Sophie barely had time to leap back onto her bed and put on what she hoped was a pitiful expression before the door opened. It was her mother.

"Don't bother pulling a long face with me," Mrs. Hartley said briskly as she dumped an armful of clean clothes onto Nora's bed. She looked at Sophie with a combination of sympathy and exasperation. "How many times have I told you? Every time you do that thing with your nose, you end up crying. If you don't have sense enough to stop, you won't get any sympathy from me.

"Come on and help me," she said as she started sorting out the laundry. "I didn't want to come up the stairs empty-handed." Her mother held up a pair of socks. "These are yours, I believe."

Sophie jumped up, took the socks, and stuffed them into her drawer. Then she took Nora's T-shirt from her mother and put it into Nora's middle drawer. Next came Sophie's jeans and Nora's sweatshirt. Before she knew it, helping her mother had made Sophie feel much better.

When they were finished, Mrs. Hartley sagged onto Nora's bed and fastened her curly hair on the top of her head with a clip she pulled from the pocket of her blouse. "This is the first time I've had a chance to sit down all day," she said in her good-natured way. "Now, what's this Nora tells me about you worrying you're not good at anything?"

Sophie sat down next to her mother and leaned against her generous side. "Mrs. Ogilvy said I was clumsy," she said. "I heard her." But it had already lost its sting. Having her mother to herself made Sophie feel contented.

"She said no such thing," said Mrs. Hartley. "And it was your own fault for wearing those shoes."

"I wish everybody would stop saying that," said Sophie.

"Well, it's true." Her mother tousled Sophie's mass of curly hair. "You're good at putting away clean clothes," she said.

"I don't want to be good at that."

"And you're very good at making mashed potatoes," said Mrs. Hartley. "That's a big help."

"You only say that so I'll make them."

"True, I tricked you into it at first," her mother admitted. "But look what happened. You became good at it."

"Who wants to be good at making mashed potatoes?" said Sophie indignantly.

"I'm sure your Uncle Ralph wishes Aunt Helen was," Mrs. Hartley said with a laugh. "He swears he broke a tooth on the lumps in hers."

"I still don't like it."

"All right, then . . . how about being kind? You're very good at that."

"I am?" said Sophie doubtfully.

"Yes, you are," her mother said firmly. "I can always count on you to help me with Maura. And you're very kind to John." She looked at Sophie and sighed. "Sometimes a bit *too* kind," she said.

"But that's just how I *am*," grumbled Sophie, "not what I'm good at. Anyway, what's so good about being kind?" It didn't feel like something she could brag about. She'd never heard of people giving kind recitals. Or winning kindness trophies.

It didn't feel like anything.

"Take it from me," her mother said in the voice of someone who knew what she was talking about. "It's a highly underrated skill. If more people practiced being kind, the world would be a better place."

"Is Nora kind?" asked Sophie.

"When it suits her."

Good. That meant she wasn't. Being kind was beginning to sound more attractive. Sophie liked the idea of being better at something than Nora was. And it was nice getting compliments from her mother. Sophie tried to drag it out a bit longer.

"It doesn't *feel* like a skill," she insisted.

"I'm afraid it will have to do." Her mother put her hands on her knees and pushed herself into a standing position with a small groan that told Sophie their time alone was up. "I've got tons more to do before I put Maura to bed."

"Nora won't think being kind is being *good* at something," Sophie said.

"Well, it is." Mrs. Hartley gathered up what was left of the clean clothes and started out of the room. "And just like any other skill, the more you practice it, the better you'll become. You can start tomorrow with Dr. Holt."

"A doctor?" Sophie said. "I'm not sick."

"No, but Dr. Holt is. She's the one I told you about. She's Mr. Spencer's mother, over on Broad Street. She's come to stay with them for a bit. I'm going to be seeing her three times a week. You can come with me tomorrow."

"I thought you said she was a grouchy old lady," said Sophie.

"It's only because she's lonely," said Mrs. Hartley. "If you're kind to her, it will cheer her up. She wants to plant a flower garden, but she can't get around anymore. Her sight's beginning to go as well. I'm sure she'll be very grateful for the help. Get ready for bed now."

"Oh, all right." Sophie gave a resigned sigh as her mother moved away down the hall. For a minute she thought about getting out a new piece of paper and starting a third list, "Things I Don't Want to Be Good At." But three lists were too many, even for Sophie.

Being kind might not be so bad, she thought as she pulled her nightgown on over her clothes. Her mother had told her that was how English people got into their bathing suits at the beach so other people wouldn't see them bare. Last summer when Nora got her bra and started making Sophie turn around while she got undressed, Sophie had decided *she* was going to be modest, too. She had quickly discovered how convenient it was to dress and undress this way. Now if her clothes weren't dirty, she didn't bother to take them off. It made getting dressed in the morning a simple matter of whipping off her nightgown.

Sophie went into the bathroom, ran a washcloth over her face, and then rubbed a bit of toothpaste on her teeth in case her mother said "Did you brush your teeth?" and made Sophie breathe into her face. By the time she finally slipped under the covers with her horse book, she was feeling very cheerful.

Helping Dr. Holt with her garden would be fun, she decided. She liked dirt and she liked worms. Last summer Dad had paid her five cents per worm to use as bait when he went fishing. This year she might be able to charge more.

Besides, she thought, growing more and more enthusiastic about the idea, lots of times old people gave children candy and good things to eat when they were grateful. If being kind meant getting food, maybe it wasn't such a bad thing to be, after all. Maybe she would start being kind to strangers on the street so presents would start arriving in the mail.

Nicest of all, she thought as she snuggled down under the covers, was that since she was good at it already, she wouldn't have to practice very hard. Not like the painful stretching she'd had to do every week at that horrible ballet. Or the way she'd had to grip so tightly with her knees when she rode a horse that her legs were left feeling sore.

Sophie sighed happily. It was lovely being so good at something that came naturally to her. She could hardly wait to start being kind.

Chapter Three

"Who's that girl?" Mrs. Hartley asked as she pulled the car into line behind the others dropping children off at school. Mrs. Hartley was a bit of an authority on the children at Sophie's school, having sent Thad and Nora there and now Sophie and John. She used to be on the PTSA and had run the spring fair four years in a row. She didn't do much of that now that she was working, but she still seemed to know who everyone was.

John scooted over Sophie as soon as she opened her door, and ran up the path with a quick wave over his shoulder for his mother. Sophie looked at the tall girl with the long dark braid standing by herself next to the fence. The girl was pinching her nose again and again as if she were about to sneeze.

"Her name's Heather," Sophie said. "She's new."

"She looks lonely, standing off to the side like that," said Mrs. Hartley.

"No one likes her," said Sophie as she struggled with the straps of her backpack. "She says we all smell."

"What a strange thing to say," her mother said. "I imagine it's because she's homesick."

"She says Mrs. Hackle's class smells like a farmyard."

"Oh, Sophie, really. The things you say," her mother said impatiently. "Hurry up or you'll be late." Sophie kissed her mother over the back of the seat and got out. "You be kind to her, do you hear me?" Mrs. Hartley called after her.

"Oh, no," wailed Sophie. "Do I have to?"

"Ask her if she wants to walk into the school with you," her mother instructed. "Look at her, poor child, waiting for someone to talk to her." She pulled away from the curb, leaving Sophie on the sidewalk with a heavy heart.

Sophie looked at Heather. Heather's nose was pointed into the air as she stared out over the heads of the children rushing past her. If she was looking around, it was only because she was hoping something better would come along, Sophie thought sourly. Something that didn't smell bad.

Sophie sighed as she trudged across the sidewalk. She wished her mother would believe her. Heather *had* told them they all smelled. She was from California. She told them all that everyone in her family was a vegetarian and that people who ate meat smelled. She claimed she could tell what anyone had eaten for dinner by the way they smelled the next morning.

The first week she was in their class, Heather had kept inching her desk to get as far away from the others as she could until she was sitting at the edge of the room by herself. She shouldn't have bothered; by the end of the week no one wanted to sit next to her, anyway.

Sophie was thinking about all of this as she slowly walked up to her. She could hear Heather's high voice as she got closer. "Chicken . . . hamburger . . ."

Heather pinched her nose especially hard as a pack of third-grade boys ran past. "Eeeuuuw . . . bacon."

Sophie thought about the hamburger with fried onions she'd had for dinner last night and, with a feeling of doom, said, "Hi, Heather."

Heather looked at her. For a few seconds her beady brown eyes bored into Sophie's without blinking, as if she was trying to look down inside the long tunnel to Sophie's stomach and see what was there. At last she gave a small sniff. Then another sniff. Sophie found she was holding her breath to see what Heather was going to say.

"Fried onions," Heather announced.

"You *can* tell," said Sophie, impressed. Heather wasn't making it up. She actually could tell what someone had eaten by their smell! Sophie was filled with envy. It was much more impressive than being able to guess someone's age the way the man at the carnival did when the Hartley family went last summer. Sophie was still indignant that she'd spent two quarters, checking to see if he could guess her weight right two times in a row even after she'd eaten a hot dog, some onion rings, and popcorn.

But then Heather said, "Wait a minute," and Sophie was filled with doubt again. The tip of Heather's nose was quivering like a bird dog's on the scent of quail. She gave a few more sniffs and then lowered the boom.

"There's something else," she said ominously.

From the sudden pinched expression on Heather's face, Sophie could tell she didn't like the "something else" one bit. Sophie took a deep breath and held it, hoping to trap her hamburger smell inside.

"Sophie! Come on!" someone yelled. Sophie's gaze darted over Heather's shoulder. Her best friend, Jenna, was standing on the front steps. Her freckles stood out in bright spots on her face the way they always did when she was mad. Sophie's other best friend, Alice, was next to her. Alice stamped her foot and gave an impatient little gesture for Sophie to join them. Now.

Sophie swallowed. She and Jenna and Alice had been best friends since the first day of school, when they discovered they were going to be in the same Daisy troop. They had agreed that they could never have secrets from one another and that they would walk into Mrs. Hackle's class together every day. The first one to arrive always waited for the other two, no matter how late it got.

Not only that, but talking to Heather was going against their number one rule: No snobs.

Sophie wasn't exactly sure what a snob was. She didn't think Jenna and Alice were, either. What they did know was *who* was a snob. Meredith Armstrong was a snob because she got to leave school early on Fridays to go to her beach house. So was Destiny Fabrey, who was always bragging about reading on a fifth-grade level.

Then there was Tyson Thomas. His father drove him to school every day in a fancy car. That definitely made Tyson a snob. Therefore, Heather, Sophie thought rapidly, who said they all smelled like animals, must be a snob, too. Judging from the expression on Jenna's and Alice's faces, Sophie could tell they couldn't *believe* she was talking to Heather.

Sophie looked back at Heather rather desperately. She would have loved to tell her she had to go, but she didn't dare breathe in Heather's direction. On the other hand, if she didn't breathe soon, she was going to fall over dead any second. Her head was getting lighter and lighter.

"It must have been that boy who walked by," Heather said finally with a little shake of her head. Sophie's shoulders sagged with relief as she let out a burst of air. Wait till she told Jenna and Alice about her close call. They could laugh about it at lunch.

Sophie was about to go and join them when Heather put an end to her plans.

"I guess you're not as bad as all the others,"

she said, making it clear from the way she looked Sophie up and down that she was a mere baby step ahead, if that. "You can eat lunch with me today."

"You're not," said Jenna.

"How could you?" asked Alice.

They huddled around Sophie as she pulled her lunch bag out of her cubbyhole, whispering to her in low, fierce voices. Jenna was mad, but Alice was hurt, Sophie could tell. Alice got hurt feelings easily, while Jenna, who had three brothers and a hide as thick as a buffalo, got mad. Right now, though, they were clearly united against her.

"I was being kind," Sophie protested.

"Kind?" said Jenna. "To a *snob*?"

"My mother told me I had to," Sophie said. "She said more people should be kind."

"That's because she's a nurse," Alice said. "Nurses are paid to be kind."

"I bet even they aren't kind to patients who are *snobs*," agreed Jenna.

"If you have a job that says you have to be

kind, that's one thing," Alice said. "But, like, I'm going to be a hairdresser. You don't expect me to be kind to *hair*, do you?"

She and Jenna laughed in such a way they might almost have been laughing at Sophie.

Sophie appealed to Jenna. "But you're going to be a vet," she said. "You're going to be kind to animals, aren't you?"

"I'm not going to eat *lunch* with them," Jenna said.

That made them all laugh, even Sophie; they were immediately friends again. They jostled against one another for a while, saying funny things. First Jenna said, "Wouldn't you like some *moooore?*" which made them laugh and then Sophie said, "Have another quacker," which made them laugh even harder. It was all feeling very normal until Heather arrived. She stood there clutching her denim lunch bag tightly against her chest with both hands and not smiling until they stopped laughing, one by one.

When they were finally quiet, staring back at her, Heather looked at Sophie, and only at Sophie, and said, "Are you coming or not?"

Then she gave a quick glance at Alice and Jenna and sniffed.

It was a tiny sniff and she only did it once. But it was enough.

Before Sophie could decide, Jenna snatched her lunch box out of her cubby and said, "Come on, Alice. We don't want to eat lunch with two *snobs*."

"But—" said Sophie.

Jenna spun on her heels and stomped off. Alice gave Sophie one last, tragic look and followed her.

"Let them go," Heather said with a satisfied little smile. "I have tons to tell you that I don't want them to hear."

Sophie followed Heather into lunch with a sinking heart.

"Basically, we never eat things with faces," said Heather. She snapped the lid back on the container that had held cucumber and bean sprouts and tomatoes and small white cubes that she told Sophie were tofu. She carefully wiped her fork on a napkin and slid it into the bag and then took out an apple. All the while she did this, she kept shooting meaningful glances at Sophie's sandwich. It was an egg salad sandwich; Sophie was enjoying it very much. Her mother had put relish in it, so it was crunchy and smooth at the same time.

"Faces?" said Sophie. She couldn't imagine what Heather was talking about. Heather had spent all lunch period telling her about meat and digestion and cruelty to animals. Sophie must have started to daydream because she didn't remember how the subject of faces had come up.

"Like your sandwich," Heather said. "I could never eat that."

Sophie held out her sandwich and looked at it with surprise. "Egg salad doesn't have a face," she said.

"Oh, no?" Heather pinched her lips together and smiled a mean little smile, as if she knew something Sophie didn't. For a second, Sophie had the unkind thought that Heather's face looked like a prune Then

Heather said, "What do you think those eggs would have become if someone hadn't killed them for a sandwich?" and Sophie suddenly was seeing the two pale yellow chicks the Hartley children had gotten for Easter a few years ago.

The Easter bunny had left a large straw basket on the steps outside the back door. The minute John pulled off the cloth that covered it, the chicks had started chirping like mad. Sophie had fallen in love with them immediately. She couldn't believe how soft they were. Or how ticklish their tiny beaks felt on her hand when they pecked for food.

Of course, within a surprisingly short time those beaks didn't feel so funny anymore; they hurt. Almost overnight, sweet chicks were replaced by scrawny chickens that stank up the mudroom, where they were kept. It turned out that one of the chicks was a rooster. When it started running after the children, pecking at their ankles, Mr. Hartley had given the chickens to a local farmer. But as Sophie sat staring at the yellow filling between two slices of white bread in her hands, she could hear their plaintive peeps loud and clear.

"Oh," she said in a faint voice. She slowly lowered her sandwich to the table. "I guess I'm not hungry anymore."

"I didn't think you would be," said Heather.

If Sophie wasn't mistaken, Heather sounded glad.

Chapter Four

"You look a little peaked," her mother said when Sophie opened the car door and slid into the front seat. "Are you feeling all right?"

"Being kind is too hard," said Sophie, slumping down.

"Most things worth doing are," her mother said brightly as she pulled out into the traffic. "John's going to play at Trevor's this afternoon. How did it go with the new girl?"

"I ate lunch with her."

"Good girl," said Mrs. Hartley. "Don't you feel better for having been nice to her?"

"No."

Mrs. Hartley laughed and started to hum

along with the music on the radio while Sophie stared at the dashboard and thought about the subject she'd been brooding about since lunch. As much as she hated to admit it, Heather had started her thinking. She was beginning to think her parents had been trying to pull the wool over her eyes her entire life.

She looked at her mother and said, "Is meatloaf cow?"

"Good heavens, Sophie, what kind of question is that?" her mother said.

"Is it?" said Sophie.

"Well, yes, I suppose in a way it is."

"I thought so," said Sophie. She brooded for a while more and then said, "Is pork cow?"

"Is pork cow?" Mrs. Hartley looked at Sophie in astonishment. "Of course not! Pork is pig!"

"Oh." Sophie thought for a minute. "What about steak? Is steak pig?"

"Good grief." For a minute it seemed that was all Mrs. Hartley could think of to say. "What do they teach you at that school?" she asked finally.

"Well, I know one thing," Sophie said grimly, crossing her arms tightly across her chest. "Chicken is chicken, and don't bother trying to hide it."

It didn't help her mood one bit that her mother laughed all the way down the Post Road.

"Here we are, then," said Mrs. Hartley. Sophie looked up as her mother pulled into the driveway of a red brick house. "There's Dr. Holt up on the porch. She has a hard time getting around, so she uses an electric wheelchair. But don't let it fool you. She's as sharp as a tack."

"I forgot we were coming here," Sophie said. "I don't want to practice being kind anymore today."

"That's what you always say, and then you complain you're not good at anything," said her mother. She opened her door and took her bag out of the back seat. "You can just pretend, then. And stop feeling sorry for yourself. Try thinking about Dr. Holt, poor woman."

Dr. Holt looked old, but she didn't look

poor, Sophie thought as she and her mother got closer. True, Sophie could see her pink scalp through her wispy white hair, and the stockings rolled up under her knees looked as if they hurt. But the way she was leaning forward with her hands on the arms of her chair, staring at them through thick glasses as they came up the path, was anything but frail. Her eyes were milky, yes, and huge. But what Sophie felt most was their fierceness.

"You're late," she said in a surprisingly strong voice. "You said you'd be here at three. It's ten after."

"I do apologize, Dr. Holt. I'm afraid I've been running behind all day," Sophie's mother said.

"You should plan better."

"I tell myself that all the time." Mrs. Hartley laughed. "How are you feeling today?" she asked, resting her hand on Dr. Holt's thin arm.

"Lousy. What'd you expect?"

Sophie waited for her mother to get mad, but she went right on acting as if Dr. Holt wasn't being rude. She put her arm around Sophie's shoulders and pulled her forward.

"Dr. Holt, this is my daughter, Sophie," Mrs. Hartley said.

The hungry way Dr. Holt turned and peered at her reminded Sophie of a vulture.

"Hello," said Sophie.

"Speak up. I can hardly hear you."

"I said, Hello!" shouted Sophie.

"That's better." Dr. Holt settled back against her chair. "If you want to get noticed in this world, you have to learn to speak up."

Sophie would have loved to speak up. It would have cheered her up enormously if she could have been as rude to Dr. Holt as Dr. Holt was being to them. Why, if she could have her way, she would turn around and walk right back down those steps and go home. She wasn't going to waste her time being kind to a mean old lady who was rude.

As if her mother could read her thoughts, she squeezed Sophie's shoulder gently. "I'm going to leave Sophie with you while I look in on a few other patients," Mrs. Hartley said. "She wants to help you with your garden."

"She wants to, or you're making her?" asked Dr. Holt. Then, before Mrs. Hartley could answer, she said, as if Sophie wasn't even there, "What's she sulking about?"

"She's not sulking, she's tired. Aren't you, Sophie?" said Mrs. Hartley. "I brought her here straight from school. We didn't even have time to stop for a snack."

"She'll live." Dr. Holt's watery eyes flitted up and down Sophie like a whip. "Looks like she's got some padding on her."

Before Sophie could say "I'd rather have padding than be a sour old thing like you!" the way she wanted to, Dr. Holt looked at her with what Sophie could have sworn was a sparkle in her eyes and said, "Made you mad, didn't I!"

Sophie's mouth dropped open with surprise.

With a loud "Ha!" Dr. Holt jiggled a lever on the handle of her chair, spun it quickly around, and glided away from them toward the ramp at the side of the house.

"Don't just stand there," she called back over her shoulder. "Let's get started on that garden."

For the second time in that long, tiring day, Sophie was too surprised to protest.

Her mother's spaghetti and meatballs cheered her up soon enough. Sophie didn't care whether the meatballs had faces or not; she popped them in her mouth with her eyes closed so she didn't have to look. They were delicious. The spaghetti was delicious, too, and the garlic bread.

For a while, everybody was too busy eating to talk. Then Nora said she wasn't going to eat any more because she didn't want to be fat for her audition in three days, and Mrs. Hartley said that if she didn't finish what was on her plate, she wasn't going to the audition. Then Nora said if she didn't get to go, she would lock herself in her room, to which Sophie said, "You'd better not lock *my* side," which made Mrs. Hartley tell her to "Just keep eating, Sophie," so Sophie took another piece of garlic bread.

As she sat there chewing happily and listening to her mother and Nora, she was glad to think that as hard as it was to be kind, she didn't have to give up eating to do it.

"Three meatballs are not going to make you fat," Mrs. Hartley was saying. "And if that's how ballet makes you feel, perhaps you'd be better off not taking it."

"Fine." Nora jabbed a meatball furiously with her fork and stuffed it in her mouth. She chewed it for a minute, then jabbed another meatball and chewed that.

"If I didn't eat, I'd fall over dead on the soccer field," said Thad. He made a muscle. "Got to get those carbs!" he shouted.

"Oh, shut up, Thad," said Nora.

"Nora . . . ," their mother said in a warning voice.

"Sorry."

"It's just a dance, Nora," Mr. Hartley said jovially. He usually stayed out of arguments between Nora and Mrs. Hartley, but Sophie saw that his plate was clean, which meant he was getting impatient for dessert. "A lovely dance you do on your tippy-toes."

"It is *not* just a dance," Nora said tightly. "It's my life."

"Oh, your life," her father scoffed good-naturedly, and then he snorted, which made Mrs. Hartley start signaling madly with her eyebrows for him to stop.

He ignored her. "A bunch of young girls running around in their underwear is your life," he said.

"Tom . . . ," implored Mrs. Hartley.

Sophie and her brothers kept eating. They were used to their father and Nora bickering. Mrs. Hartley said they both had short fuses. That was her diplomatic way of explaining they both got mad easily. Mr. Hartley's idea of helping was to crack jokes, which always ended up making Nora mad. Then when she talked back to him, *he* got mad.

Sophie was glad she had a long fuse herself.

"They're called tutus, as if you didn't know," Nora said.

That was a mistake. Mr. Hartley's face split into a grin. "Tutus!" he cried. "How serious can you be about a sport that requires tutus?"

When John said, "Too-too!" like a train and Thad and Mr. Hartley laughed, Mrs. Hartley stood up. "Thad. John. Clear the dishes," she said. She untied Maura's bib and lifted her out of her high chair. "Sophie, take Maura into the den and play with her for a while, that's a good girl."

Sophie was glad to get away. Nora and her parents were just going to argue for a bit more, and then Nora would storm up to their room. She didn't cry, Nora, but she could slam a door with more emotion than anyone else in the family.

Sophie carried Maura into the den, where she built towers out of blocks and let Maura knock them down. Then she put on some music and leapt around the room while Maura jiggled up and down on her bottom. When they were both tired of that, Sophie got a book and pulled Maura onto her lap. Maura stuck her thumb in her mouth, and Sophie began to read. With Maura's solid weight resting trustingly against her, Sophie couldn't help thinking how much easier it was to be kind to someone who couldn't talk.

Chapter Five

"Peanut butter and jelly, please," said Sophie.

"What, again?" her mother said with surprise. She held the knife covered with mayonnaise poised in the air over a slice of bread. "No tuna fish today?"

"Peanut butter and jelly." Sophie sighed.

"My goodness," said Mrs. Hartley. She put the knife down and opened the cupboard door. "Ever since the day we ran out of cereal last week and I had to give you all peanut butter sandwiches for breakfast, you've asked for it every day, Sophie. You never even used to like peanut butter. Get the jelly out for me, that's a good girl."

Sophie did, and then rested her elbows on the counter and her chin on her hands while she watched her mother slather peanut butter on one piece of bread and jelly on the other. When Mrs. Hartley turned away to pull a sandwich bag out of a drawer, Sophie quickly dunked her finger in the jar and stuck a wad of peanut butter in her mouth.

"Any more of that and I'll have to send you back up to brush your teeth," Mrs. Hartley said as she turned back around. "You did brush your teeth, didn't you?" she asked, looking Sophie hard in the face.

Sophie breathed at her.

"Peanut butter," said Mrs. Hartley.

That's exactly what Heather had said the morning Sophie ate the peanut butter sandwich for breakfast. It was a few days after they had eaten lunch together for the first time. Jenna and Alice had stopped waiting for Sophie in their usual spot, so she was walking into school as slowly as she could, trying to think how she was going to hide her chicken breath from Heather, when Heather jumped out in front of her.

Sophie was so startled she forgot to cover her mouth, which was the only idea she had come up with, and blurted out, "Hi, Heather!"

"Peanut butter," said Heather. She smiled the biggest smile Sophie had ever seen on her face. "I love peanut butter," she said. Then she said, "Oh, Sophie!" in such a way it made Sophie feel as if she had given Heather a present of some kind. "I almost like you a lot," said Heather.

Heather talked about it all during lunch. About smells and pores and how the smell of what a person ate oozed out of them all over their body. Sophie thought it sounded very strange, but Heather said that if Sophie ate enough peanut butter, she would not only smell of it when she talked, but even when she walked. She made it sound like a wonderful thing and beamed at Sophie as if she really liked her.

Sophie was amazed to see what a change a few days of kindness could make in a person. But even though she was glad Heather was happy, Sophie wasn't at all happy herself. She missed eating with her friends.

"I'll go get Jenna and Alice," she said at one point, recklessly interrupting Heather's lecture. "They'd love to hear about all of this."

Heather stopped and pursed her lips to let Sophie know she was being rude. "Not yet," she said. She gave a delicate little sniff. "I'm allergic. My nose is still too sensitive."

"Your nose?" said Sophie.

It seemed that Heather's nose missed California. It needed time to get used to Ohio, she said. The air in California was so much cleaner; her nose needed time to adapt. Sophie, who had listened to her father rant about the smog in California every time he had to move a family out there, thought maybe Heather had it backwards. But she wasn't about to get Heather started on air in addition to smells. And food. She kept quiet.

"Maybe I could try in a few weeks," Heather said. "But then," she added quickly, "only one at a time."

For one desperate second Sophie considered crying. Or even just letting tears well up in her eyes to let Heather know how disappointed she was. But almost the minute the idea came to her, it died. If she saw tears, Heather would only think that Sophie had allergies, too. It would give them even more in common than she thought they had now.

Then, of course, judging from the way Jenna and Alice had been acting the past few days, Sophie was pretty sure they didn't want to be Heather's friends. Or even Sophie's anymore. They were actually being very mean about it, she thought indignantly. Every time she had tried to talk to them, they'd turned their backs on her. She thought that maybe if she could get Alice alone, she could get her to talk. But Jenna was always by Alice's side. It was beginning to feel very unfair to Sophie that she was the only one who was trying to be kind.

She was thinking about the problem as she

watched her mother put the sandwich in her lunch box. At least eating peanut butter sandwiches every day had given her one less thing to worry about; Heather had stopped sniffing around her like a guard dog. She couldn't help wondering, though, if maybe peanut butter was starting to give her bad thoughts.

"That's a very big sigh," her mother said. "Are you sure you don't want to switch with John? He won't mind."

"That's okay. At least I won't smell like meatloaf."

"Really, Sophie," said Mrs. Hartley. "You say the strangest things."

"We should be about fifteen minutes," said Mrs. Hartley. "I'll send Dr. Holt out when we're through if she's feeling up to it."

Sophie ran around to the backyard. The gardening tools were still lying where she had left them two days earlier. She dropped to her knees at the edge of the flower bed and picked up a trowel. It was lovely to be out here by herself; she dug away at the soil for a while, finding plenty of worms and dropping them into the coffee can her father had given her that morning.

"All right, you win," he had told her as he climbed into the cab of his truck. "Seven cents a worm, but not a penny more. I still say it's highway robbery." He gave two short blasts on the truck's horn, and was gone.

As she worked, Sophie quickly realized that adding sevens was going to be much harder than adding fives. She hated the sevens times table. And the eights. The nines, too, if she was being truthful. But the tens were easy—all you did was add a zero—so she counted off the worms by tens and lined up a stick on the grass for every group of ten she found. She could figure out exactly how much money her dad owed her when she got home.

She had three sticks so far, and was happily working away when she heard a door open behind her and a too-familiar voice say, "Your mother said she'll be back in half an hour."

Dr. Holt came rolling across the terrace toward her and stopped just short of the grass. "I wouldn't do it that way if I were you," she said shortly.

Sophie sat back on her heels. "What way?" she asked.

"Digging a trench like that. That's not the way it's done."

"I'm not planting the flowers yet," Sophie said. "I'm looking for worms."

"What do you need worms for?" said Dr. Holt.

"My dad said . . ." Sophie stopped. She suddenly felt very odd. This morning it didn't feel as if there was anything wrong with taking worms out of Dr. Holt's garden. But she didn't like the way Dr. Holt was looking at her. It made her feel as if she was doing something wrong.

"Well, what did your father say?" Dr. Holt said impatiently.

"He said he'd give me seven cents a worm," Sophie said.

"And who said you could sell my worms?" said Dr. Holt. She sat up straight and glared down her nose at Sophie like a judge in a courtroom. "Were you going to give me a cut of the profit, or keep it all for yourself?"

It *did* sort of sound like a crime the way Dr. Holt put it. Sophie suddenly felt guilty. That wasn't the way she had meant it at all. It was mean of Dr. Holt to make her feel so bad. Sophie could tell she was enjoying it, too.

"Worms don't belong to people," Sophie said stiffly.

"Whom *do* they belong to?"

Sophie didn't want to say she thought they belonged to God; Dr. Holt would probably make it sound silly. But she wasn't going to stand here, either, being glared at as if she was a criminal.

"Fine." Sophie turned the can upside down and dumped the worms into a squirming pile on the soil. "You can keep your silly old worms," she said. "You're a mean old lady to call me a thief."

"I never said any such thing," said Dr. Holt.

"Well, that's how you made me feel." Sophie started picking things up—the trowel, the rake, anything she could find. She didn't know what she was going to do with it all. But standing here in front of Dr. Holt was horrible.

She clanged everything together as noisily as she could so she wouldn't have to talk. She was tired of being kind. It didn't work, anyway. All it did was get her in deeper and deeper trouble. First Heather. Now Dr. Holt. She was sick of it.

When she couldn't hold another thing, Sophie turned back around.

Dr. Holt was looking down at her lap, picking away at the fabric of her skirt with her gnarly hand. When the clanking noises stopped, she turned and looked at the side of the house, as if looking at bricks would be better than looking at Sophie. "Well, then, I'm sorry," she said in a stiff voice.

It was so surprising, it stopped Sophie cold. Dr. Holt hated to apologize, she could tell. So when she finally did, she really meant it. It was so much like Nora, Sophie stopped feeling mad immediately.

"I suppose this means you're going to quit," Dr. Holt said to the bricks in a gruff voice.

"I don't know," Sophie said slowly. That was surprising, too. She couldn't quit; her mother would be angry at her. The rest of the family would laugh at her, too, when she told them about the worms. And then, of course, she would have to add "kind" to the list of things she wasn't good at just when the list of things she was good at seemed to be catching up.

But it was nice to think Dr. Holt would miss her if she did quit. Sophie could tell from Dr. Holt's voice that she would. Anyway, it was fun planting flowers. Sophie liked it. And sometimes—only sometimes—talking to Dr. Holt was interesting.

"You've never even given me anything to eat," said Sophie.

That made Dr. Holt look at her. "You never asked."

"Asking's not polite."

"You're absolutely right," said Dr. Holt. "All right, then . . ." She spun her chair around so that she faced the house. "Let's go get something to eat." She started moving. "Strawberry shortcake all right with you?" she called.

"Oh, yes," said Sophie.

"I made it myself," said Dr. Holt. She stopped her chair and waited while Sophie dumped her armload of tools in a corner of the terrace and opened the door. "I bet that surprises you."

"I can't imagine you making anything sweet," admitted Sophie.

"First, you call me a mean old lady, and then you tell me I'm a sour old goat," grumbled Dr. Holt.

"I never said any such thing," said Sophie.

"Ha!" Dr. Holt shot her an amused glance as she rolled past her into the house. "You're a fresh kid. I don't know why I'm even cooking for you."

But Sophie knew why: she had earned it.

The strawberry shortcake was sweet, very sweet. She ate two pieces.

Sophie tried not to watch Nora making bird faces at herself in their mirror after dinner, but it was impossible not to. She pretended she was doing her spelling homework, which her mother had threatened to start testing her on if she didn't work harder, but she was really keeping a close eye on Nora.

First, Nora would crane her head one way and lift her chin in the air to see what she looked like out of the corner of her eye. Then she craned it around the other way and did the same thing. Sometimes she pushed her lips out as if she was about to kiss someone.

She was trying to see which was her better profile. Sophie knew, because she did the same thing. But while Sophie was always checking to see how she was going to look with a tiara, she knew that Nora was imagining how she was going to look with a wreath of beautiful white feathers on her head when she danced the role of the swan in her ballet performance. It was the lead role; Nora wanted it more than anything. She hadn't said as much to Sophie, but Sophie knew. There was only one other girl in Nora's class who might get it. Her name was Lauren.

Lauren used to help teach the beginners' class. She was the oldest girl in the school, two years older than Nora. She was taller than Nora, too, which mattered in ballet. Her straight blond hair was always pulled back into a perfect chignon at the nape of her neck that never came unraveled. Her shoulder blades stood out under her leotard and her legs were as long and thin as a colt's. Even her fingers were thin.

All the little girls in Sophie's ballet class started out wanting to be just like Lauren. Sophie had, too. But then something about the way Lauren looked at her and talked to her had made Sophie stop wishing she could dance as well as Lauren and started making her realize she'd never be as good. No matter how hard she tried. Sophie didn't know how Lauren did it, but she could still remember the feeling.

It wasn't simply that Lauren wasn't kind, Sophie realized, it was that Lauren was mean. She was suddenly very worried for her sister. It gave her a terrible feeling in her stomach to see the way Nora's damp hair was curling around her face, even though she had it pulled back into a pony tail. Hair mattered, too, in ballet, Sophie thought. Tall snobs with straight hair would be very hard to compete with.

She felt the surge of fierce protectiveness she always felt when an outsider was mean to anyone in her family. It was one thing when her brothers and sisters were mean to one another, but another thing altogether when someone else was. Sophie felt she just *had* to say something to make Nora feel better.

"Who cares if Lauren is taller than you and has straighter hair?" she blurted out loyally. "Your nose looks much more like a beak."

It didn't seem to comfort Nora at all. She whirled around to Sophie with a furious face.

"Why are you looking at me?" she shouted. "I told you not to look at me! You're always spying on me! I can't stand it! I can't even get any privacy in my own room!"

"It's my room, too," said Sophie. "And I wasn't spying. I was looking around."

"Looking around?" cried Nora. "At what? It's our bedroom. What is there to look at?" Nora's hair was flying out around her head now, but Sophie didn't think this was the right time to suggest she might need to use more spray. "Oh . . . oh . . ." Nora seemed stuck, like a windup toy against a rug. Then she came unstuck. "Oh, I hate you, Sophie!" she cried. "I hate you, I hate you, I hate you!" She yanked her bathrobe off the hook on the closet door, opened the door to the hall, and ran out of the room. When Sophie heard the bathroom door slam, she fell back against her pillow and sighed.

It was really very interesting. Whenever Nora yelled that she hated her, she always yelled it in threes. But when she just spoke it, she only said it once. As in, "I hate you, Sophie," when Sophie took the last cookie. Or the last card from the deck. Nora had said it to her so often, it didn't really mean anything anymore. But there was no doubt Nora was mad at her.

Sophie sighed again. Their mother always told them it was better to get angry and clear the air than to walk around brooding. She said that people who let things get pent up inside only ended up making themselves sick.

If that was true, Nora must be feeling pretty cleaned out by now, Sophie thought. Judging from the sound of that door, Nora had definitely moved from brooding to mad.

She bet Nora would thank her someday.

Probably not tonight, but soon.

Sophie briefly considered taking out her list and finally adding "Being kind" to the top of the things she was good at. But then she thought it would be too much like bragging, so she decided to wait. Then she could add "Being modest" to the list, too. All in all, it was very satisfying to think how quickly her second list was catching up to her first.

Chapter Six

"How about today?" Sophie asked hopefully. "You'd really like them if you actually talked to them."

Sophie kept her eyes on Heather's face. She didn't have to look down at the other end of the table to know that Alice and Jenna were glaring at her. That's what they had been doing for days. Every time Sophie smiled at them, they mouthed "snob" and looked the other away.

Even though they were her best friends, she was getting tired of them. She was getting tired of Heather, too. It felt as if everybody was allowed to go around acting however they wanted except for her.

"Not yet," Heather said briskly. "They don't have enough points."

"Points?" said Sophie.

"It's the system we used at my school in California," said Heather. She took a small notebook and a pencil out of her lunch bag and opened it. "I need to teach you about it. It's really the best way to keep track of who you want to be friends with."

"Oh," said Sophie. This was going to be long and complicated, like food and smells, she could tell. As she watched Heather run her finger down her list of names, she thought that life in California didn't sound anything like life in Ohio. Heather's list looked alarmingly long from upside down. All the names had little boxes next to them. Some of the boxes had check marks. Many more didn't.

"You have four points so far," Heather explained. "You got two points for eating onions, one point for not having bushy eyebrows. . . ."

Heather looked up at her. "I hate bushy eyebrows. Don't you?" she said, and then, before Sophie could answer, looked at her list again as she ran her finger further down the page and said, "and one point for being in the same reading group I am. That's four. Four is the minimum number you need to be someone's friend."

Minimum number? Sophie didn't even know what a minimum number was. She'd never heard about points before, either. And why did she get two points for eating onions and nothing for peanut butter when Heather loved it so much?

It was all too confusing.

"I'm afraid Jenna and Alice have only one point each," Heather told her. She said it regretfully, like a doctor delivering bad news. "Jenna's only in the blue reading group, and Alice can't do cursive."

"I can't do cursive, either," said Sophie.

"True, but you knew the capital of Oklahoma yesterday. It evens out." Heather looked down again and started checking off boxes with sharp, choppy strokes while Sophie watched. The list of Heather's friends was getting shorter and shorter. Unfortunately, if Sophie went on eating lunch with Heather much longer, it was going to be *her* friend list, too. There wasn't another member of Mrs. Hackle's class sitting anywhere near them.

But there didn't seem to be anything Sophie could do about it.

She had four points.

"Some people," Heather said to her disgustedly. "Chris Brooks has such huge ears. And Allie North wears clothes that don't match."

"Clothes should always match," said Sophie.

Heather looked up at her. "You'd never wear stripes with checks, would you?"

Sophie panicked. She wore anything with anything, as long as it fit.

"Of course, you wouldn't," Heather answered for her. She looked back at her list. "No one does."

"Oh."

"And what about Tamara Wilson?" said Heather, looking up again.

It was a little bit like being interrogated: Sophie knew there was a right answer but she didn't know what it was. And she wasn't about to take a guess.

"What about her?" she said cautiously. She was rapidly realizing that it didn't matter if none of Heather's answers made any sense to her. She didn't have to understand Heather's rules. She only had to follow them.

"She wears socks with sandals, that's what," said Heather. "No one wears socks with sandals in California."

"But we live in Ohio," said Sophie.

"It doesn't matter. Rules are rules." Heather clapped her notebook shut and leaned across the table with a strange look in her eyes that made Sophie nervous. She couldn't tell whether Heather was going to kiss her or bite her. She leaned back ever so slightly.

"One more point," Heather said to her breathlessly, "and we'll be best friends."

Dr. Holt was in a bad mood again, Sophie could tell. If she was *always* in a bad mood, that would be one thing, Sophie thought resentfully as she dragged a bag of soil across the grass. Sophie would know what to expect. But Dr. Holt was in a different mood every day, depending on what kind of night she'd had. It made it very hard for Sophie to know how to act.

She had just planted the red flowers next to the yellow flowers because she thought it would look pretty. But then Dr. Holt said she wanted them next to the white ones, so Sophie had to dig them up. Next, she had tried to make a fancy pattern with the pink ones along the wall. Dr. Holt told her they were crooked.

"Don't try taking advantage of me because of my eyes," she said irritably, plucking at the sweater draped around her shoulders. "I'm not blind yet. I can still tell a straight line."

"That's not what I was doing," said Sophie. "I thought it would look nice."

"You dig the holes," said Dr. Holt. "I'll tell you what to put in them."

"I'm not just here to take orders, you know," muttered Sophie.

"What'd you say?"

"Nothing." Sophie plunged her trowel into the soil and pulled it back out so fast that a shower of dirt flew up, sprinkling her knees, the terrace, and Dr. Holt's shoes.

"Hey! Watch what you're doing there, toots!" said Dr. Holt.

"Don't call me 'toots,'" said Sophie.

"Then don't you go making a mess of my daughter's terrace." Dr. Holt shook her feet in the air to knock the dirt off, but some of it stayed on, caught up in little clumps in her shoelaces. It served her right, Sophie thought meanly. She could feel Dr. Holt sitting there, angry and proud. Sophie wondered how proud she would be if she knew there was dirt all over her shoes.

"I can get someone else to do this, you know," Dr. Holt said in a stiff voice. "You don't have to do me any favors."

"And *you* don't have to be so grouchy all the time," said Sophie. She started on another hole.

"You'd be grouchy, too, if you were losing

your sight and couldn't get around without a wheelchair."

"It's not *my* fault," said Sophie. "It's not anyone's fault."

"I know it's not, but it makes me mad."

"Well, you don't have to get mad at *me*."

The air between them seemed to get a little lighter after they said this. Sophie worked in silence for a while. Then she couldn't stand it any longer.

"You've got a bit of dirt . . . ," she said, and reached out and brushed the dirt off Dr. Holt's shoe with her hand.

"Thank you," said Dr. Holt.

"You're welcome."

Sophie worked some more in silence. "Why don't you fix yourself if you're a doctor?" she said finally.

"I'm not a medical doctor, I'm a doctor of history," said Dr. Holt.

"What's history?" said Sophie.

"The story of things that happened in the past."

"What good can a doctor do if it already

happened?" said Sophie. "It's too late to fix it, isn't it?"

"Ha! You can say that again." Sophie wasn't sure, but it looked as if Dr. Holt thought Sophie had said something funny. "I'm called a doctor because I studied so much about it," Dr. Holt went on. "I taught English history to girls in a boarding school for almost forty years."

"Oh."

"You might have enjoyed it," said Dr. Holt. "I told them stories about kings and queens—"

"Queens?" Sophie's head shot up. "Queens . . . who wore tiaras?"

"You like that idea, do you?" Dr. Holt smiled, as if she was actually glad she'd pleased Sophie; it changed her whole face. Sophie found herself smiling back.

"English history is full of queens who wore tiaras," said Dr. Holt. "I could tell you about a girl who became queen when she wasn't much older than you are."

"Really?" said Sophie.

"Queen Victoria. She was crowned queen of

England when she was only eighteen years old."

"Oh." Sophie couldn't help but sound disappointed. "That's much older than me."

"She was a princess when she was thirteen," said Dr. Holt. "Is that close enough?"

"It's better," Sophie admitted. Then, "Did she wear a tiara?"

"*Did* she? You've never seen so many diamonds."

"Ohhh . . ." Sophie had never heard anything so wonderful in her whole life. She pictured a young princess of thirteen wearing a magnificent tiara sparkling with diamonds. *Real* diamonds.

"Did she wear it all day, every day?" she asked reverently.

"She had to. She was the queen."

"Except when she was riding, right?"

"Riding?" That seemed to stump Dr. Holt. She leaned back in her chair and rubbed her chin. "Well, she rode horses a lot. I should think she wore it even when she was riding."

"I don't see how she could have," Sophie

said practically. "I rode. All you do is bounce up and down from the minute you get on the horse until the minute you get off. It's awful. You'd have to tie a tiara down with string."

"String? On a queen?" said Dr. Holt. "You mean a gold chain, don't you?"

"Of course," breathed Sophie. She was carried away by the very thought of it. The gold, the diamonds. "Oh, I hope I meet a queen someday," she said wistfully.

"You'll have learn how to curtsy first," said Dr. Holt. "Queens don't shake hands with commoners."

"What's a commoner?"

"You are. I am. Anyone who's not a member of the royal family is considered a commoner."

"That doesn't sound like a very nice thing to call us," said Sophie.

"That's neither here nor there," Dr. Holt said firmly. "If you want to meet a queen, you'll have to learn how to curtsy."

"But how?" said Sophie. "I don't know anyone who knows how to curtsy."

"I do."

"You *do?*" Sophie said. Dr. Holt was getting more and more amazing all the time. She couldn't imagine anyone as stiff as Dr. Holt curtsying. Or letting anyone call her a commoner. Not even a queen.

"I can teach you, too," said Dr. Holt. Then before Sophie could say another word, she added, "But I'm warning you, it's hard work. There's a lot more to curtsying than just bobbing up and down."

"That's all right," Sophie said rashly, thinking that her mother would fall over dead in a faint if she could hear. "I love hard work."

Chapter Seven

And hard work it was. Sophie was so eager to start that Dr. Holt agreed they could put the gardening to one side for a while. Sophie didn't even mind the way Dr. Holt sat barking orders at her. She tried to follow her instructions very carefully. If she could get it right and meet a queen, Sophie was confident the tiara wouldn't be far behind.

It was much more complicated than she'd thought. There were a ton of things she had to remember. Back straight, arms out, head up, toes pointing straight ahead. The hardest part was keeping her balance. The first few tries, every time Sophie got halfway into a curtsy, she fell over.

"It's not a bob, the way all you young people seem to think it is these days," Dr. Holt said unsympathetically as Sophie collapsed into another heap on the grass. "A real curtsy is a dignified, elegant movement. You *lower* your body to the ground. You don't drop it."

"How can I be dignified if I don't even know what it means?" Sophie grumbled, getting to her feet.

"Believe me," said Dr. Holt, "you'll know what it means when you get it right."

Unfortunately, Sophie's body didn't want to lower, it wanted to drop. No matter how hard she tried. "You're wobbling," said Dr. Holt. "That's because you're leaning forward too much."

"I can't help it," Sophie wailed as she fell onto the grass for what felt like the thousandth time. She lay on her back and looked up at the sky, discouraged. "When I get the back right, you tell me my legs are wrong.

When I get the legs right, you tell me my arms wrong."

"You're not giving up, are you?"

Sophie heard the challenge in Dr. Holt's voice. She thought that maybe her life would be easier if she wanted a baseball cap, say, instead of a tiara.

But she didn't.

"No," she said resignedly.

"Then stand up and try it again."

Sophie sighed and stood up.

"Slowly now," Dr. Holt told her. "Remember: You've just walked down a long red carpet; you're standing in front of the queen; she's up on her throne wearing an ermine cloak and a magnificent tiara."

Sophie didn't know what ermine was, but it sounded romantic. She stood up straighter.

"Good. Now, right foot forward . . . that's right. Have some dignity. Chin held high . . . hands out to the sides holding your magnificent silk gown . . . no smiling, Sophie. The queen doesn't like it."

Sophie frowned obediently.

"You don't have to look as if you're mad at her," said Dr. Holt. "That's better. Now, carefully . . . carefully! Back straight . . . Slowly *lower* your body until your left knee almost touches the ground. That's it. Now hold just a moment, and come back up."

Wobbling only the tiniest bit, Sophie made it back up into a standing position.

"Now you're cooking!" said Dr. Holt. She looked as if she would have jumped up out of her chair if she'd been able to. "It took you long enough, but you look pretty good."

Sophie was beaming. "Pretty good" from Dr. Holt was like "Bravo!" from anyone else. She'd done it. It was funny how much more a compliment meant when the person giving it to you was usually a grouch.

After that, she didn't want to stop curtsying. The more she practiced, the steadier she got. Her favorite part was the slow dip of her head she had to make when her knee was touching the ground. The tiny nod that said, "Your Majesty."

It made Sophie feel elegant. She could

almost hear the queen saying back, "Sophie."

She practiced it so many more times that Dr. Holt started to get a little grouchy again, so Sophie went back to gardening. She could hardly wait to get home and practice in front of the mirror. She wasn't going to tell anyone in her family about it until she could do it perfectly. Especially Nora.

She would use a book on her head. She'd hate it if her tiara slipped down over her nose in front of the queen.

As soon as she had helped with the dishes after dinner, Sophie ran up to her room and shut the door. She took off her sneakers and put on her velvet shoes and then, because she didn't own an ermine cloak, slipped her nightgown over her head and tied a towel around her neck before placing the book on her head. But no matter how slowly she moved, the book kept slipping off and thumping on the floor, so Sophie took it off in case the noise made anyone come up to see what she was doing.

She soon discovered that if she watched

herself in the mirror while she curtsied, she wobbled too much, especially when her knee was near the floor. So she lined her stuffed animals up in a row on her bed and curtsied to them. They didn't clap or show any signs of appreciation, though, so Sophie began to wish there was someone in her family she could curtsy to without being laughed at.

When she heard her mother say good night to John in his room across the hall, she knew it was eight o'clock. The Hartley children went to bed at half-hour intervals, starting with Maura, who went at seven-thirty. That meant Sophie had half an hour more to practice before her mother came up to check on her.

Sophie opened her door a crack to see whether John's door was still open. It was. The minute he saw her, John scrambled out of bed and scooted over to lie on his stomach next to his door. Sophie often entertained him from her doorway at night when he was supposed to be asleep. He was a very good audience.

"Now, imagine you're the queen," Sophie instructed him.

"Boys can't be the queen," said John.

"The king, then."

"Off with her head!" John shouted in a loud whisper, waving his arm as if he were brandishing a sword.

"John . . ."

John quieted down and watched patiently while Sophie did a whole string of curtsies. Then he said, "It's getting a little boring," so she got a belt from her drawer and looped it around a stuffed sheep on her bed and dragged it behind her as she marched around her room, quietly singing *Mary Had a Little Lamb* and then curtsying. She was halfway through her final curtsy when she heard footsteps on the stairs. John made a dash for his bed, and Sophie fell over sideways.

It was Nora.

"What are you doing?" she said. She stepped coldly over Sophie's body as if it were nothing more than a lumpy sack of potatoes, went over to her dresser, and picked up her hairbrush.

"Resting," said Sophie.

"Well, go rest downstairs," Nora said. She began brushing her hair. "I need to rehearse."

Sophie could have argued that it was *her* time in the bedroom and that Nora had no right to tell her to leave. But she was feeling generous because of how well her curtsying was going. Besides, she thought Nora's face looked very pale.

"I'll watch you if you want," she offered as she sat up. "I can tell you what you're doing wrong."

"As if you'd know," said Nora.

"But I could—"

"I don't want your help." Nora put down her hairbrush and turned around. "You don't know anything, Sophie. Just go away and leave me alone. And you can take your babyish animals with you." She snatched Sophie's sheep off the floor and tossed it out into the hall. "I'm sick of them."

It was one thing for Nora to be mean to her, but to take it out on an innocent sheep? Sophie ran into the hall and picked up the sheep, cradling it in her arms as if it were taking its last breath. When their bedroom door slammed shut behind her, she whirled around.

"I do, too, know something, Nora!" she yelled, pounding on the door a few times for good measure. "I'm better at being bad at ballet than you are, so there!"

Her storming down the stairs was anything but queenly.

". . . and then she threw Curly against the wall."

"Who's Curly?" said Mrs. Hartley.

"My sheep."

"Oh, Sophie." Mrs. Hartley's face was red from the steam that shot up from the iron when she set it down. There was a warm, friendly smell of steam and clean clothes in the kitchen. "Try to be nice to her," her mother said. "It's only for two more days."

"I *was* trying to be nice," said Sophie. "She was still mean."

"It's because she's worried," her mother said.

"Then why doesn't she act worried?"

"Pride," said Mrs. Hartley. "Many times, people are too proud to show how they really feel, so they act mean."

"That's no excuse," said Sophie. She thought about Dr. Holt. "They act mean when they're sick, too."

"Right."

"And homesick," she said, thinking about Heather. "They want people to be nice to them, but then they take advantage of them. That's what *you* always say," she said defensively, seeing the expression on her mother's face.

"You're right, I do," said Mrs. Hartley. "My goodness. You're becoming a regular philosopher."

"And Nora's not a prima ballerina," Sophie said. "She's a prima donna."

It made her feel very proud the way her mother suddenly plunked the iron on its base and stared at her through a rush of steam. "Wherever did you learn that expression?" she asked. "Are you *sure* you're the real Sophie Hartley?"

"Dr. Holt told me," said Sophie. "She knows lots of interesting things."

"Like what?" said Mrs. Hartley.

"Oh, history and things," Sophie said vaguely. She wished she could tell her mother about curtsying and meeting a queen and everything, but she couldn't.

Not yet.

"So she's not just a grouchy old lady anymore," said her mother.

"She still is, but I'm working on her."

"Now that," her mother said, "is something I'd like to see."

Chapter Eight

"Bad news," said Heather. She slid into the seat next to Sophie and looked at her mournfully.

"What?" Sophie said.

"Destiny Fabrey is catching up to you. We were both just promoted to the gold reading group, and you weren't." Heather's mouth turned down. "That means she gets two more points."

"Oh, no," said Sophie, feeling her heart give a great leap into the air and fly joyously around.

"That's not all," said Heather solemnly as

she opened her notebook. "You lost a point this morning for peanut butter."

"I thought you loved peanut butter," said Sophie.

"Not when it's on people's clothes," said Heather. She looked meaningfully at a spot in the middle of Sophie's chest. Sophie looked down. A generous dollop of peanut butter was smudged around a button on her shirt.

"Oh, no," Sophie said again.

Heather was busy making checks in her notebook and disapproving *tsk-tsk* noises with her tongue. When she finally looked back up, Sophie could tell the verdict wasn't good.

"I didn't tell you because I didn't want to get your hopes up. Sometimes these things don't stick." Heather could have been talking Russian for all Sophie understood. "You moved up to five at the end of school yesterday when you got a ninety-five on the spelling test." She heaved a mighty sigh. "You were actually my best friend for the entire night until this morning."

"I was?" said Sophie. She immediately thought how glad she was she hadn't known.

She doubted whether she would have been able to sleep.

"Now, I'm sad to say, it's even." Sophie didn't think Heather sounded sad; she sounded glad. "Destiny had two, and now she has four," she said. "And because of the peanut butter problem you're back down to four, too. Whoever gets another point first gets to be my best friend."

"Either that," said Sophie, "or whoever loses a point first, doesn't."

Dr. Holt wasn't at all interested in seeing how much Sophie's curtsy had improved.

"No more dilly-dallying," she said irritably when Sophie offered to show her. "Too many more nights like the one I had last night and I'm not going to live long enough see this garden finished. Let's get going."

Sophie's feelings were a little hurt, but she dutifully picked up a pot of purple flowers and carried it onto the last empty spot in the flower bed. Then she picked up a pot of blue flowers and put it next to it.

"What do you think you're doing?" snapped Dr. Holt. "Purple doesn't go next to blue."

"I think it looks pretty," said Sophie.

"Then you must be colorblind. It looks terrible."

Sophie took a deep breath. "Different people have different opinions," she said.

"Not when they're working in my garden," said Dr. Holt. "I'm the boss here."

Sophie put down the trowel. She was tired of arguing with Dr. Holt; there was no way she was ever going to win. Dr. Holt blamed her grouchiness on how sick she was when what she really was, was rude. Dr. Holt was a bully, Sophie decided. And Sophie was sick of it.

She suddenly knew what dignified meant, too; it meant acting calm, even when what you wanted to do was stamp your feet and yell.

Sophie stood up, brushed off her knees, and went and stood in front of Dr. Holt's chair.

"Well, what are you waiting for?" said Dr. Holt.

Sophie put her left foot on the grass behind her and held out her imaginary silk gown.

With her chin in the air and her back straight, she slowly and graciously lowered her body until she felt the tip of the grass scratch against her knee. One quick nod to Dr. Holt, and she rose to her feet again.

Then she stood there, waiting.

"What was that for?" Dr. Holt said in a querulous voice. She glared at Sophie with her fierce eyes as if trying to scare her off, but Sophie didn't budge. She knew what it was for; Sophie could tell she knew.

She didn't say a word.

"Ha!" said Dr. Holt.

This time, Sophie was absolutely *sure* there was a gleam in her eyes. "Bet you can't do it again," said Dr. Holt.

Sophie did do it again. A perfect, dignified curtsy.

Then she stared back at Dr. Holt in stubborn silence. It seemed to go on for quite a long time.

"Oh, all right. Have it your own way," Dr. Holt said at last. She waved a hand toward the pots. "Put blue next to purple. See if I care."

"Thank you," said Sophie. She picked up another pot of flowers and put it down in the bed. Then another pot. Purple, blue, purple, blue. She stood back to take a look. "There. Doesn't that look beautiful?" she asked.

"Magnificent," said Dr. Holt.

Sophie set about digging a hole for each plant. "Isn't it much nicer when we don't argue?" she said conversationally.

"We're still arguing," said Dr. Holt. "We're just not doing it out loud."

"I hope Dr. Holt's not being too hard on you," Mrs. Hartley said on the drive home. She sounded worried. "Her daughter said she had quite a reputation for whipping her students into shape when she taught school." She gave Sophie a quick glance. "She might have some old-fashioned ideas about how she wants you to treat her."

"She's all right," said Sophie. "Sometimes she's a little grouchy, that's all."

Her mother drove for a while, looking thoughtful. Then, "Didn't I see you curtsying to her out there this afternoon?" she said finally when they came to a red light. "I just happened to be looking out the window."

Sophie nodded. "I was teaching her how to be polite."

Her mother sat up straighter and turned to look at her. It made Sophie feel even more satisfied than she'd been feeling when she first got in the car. She'd wanted to tell her mother about what had happened, but she wasn't sure how. The fact that her mother had been spying on her made it easier.

"You?" her mother said. "Teaching *her?*"

"Yep."

"And you did that by curtsying to her?"

"Talking back was getting me nowhere," said Sophie. "Then I wondered what Queen Victoria would do." She looked at her mother. "Do you know about Queen Victoria? The teenaged queen?"

"I've never heard her referred to that way before," her mother said. "But, yes. A bit."

"Queen Victoria was never mean to anyone, or yelled at them," Sophie said. "She didn't have to." She wasn't exactly sure if this was true, but she'd been thinking about it quite a bit. She couldn't imagine a queen sitting on her throne, arguing. Not in an ermine cloak. She acted so dignified that everyone acted dignified back. If they didn't, she waved her magic wand and made them disappear.

Sophie thought maybe she was mixing her facts up a bit, but she liked the way it sounded. "If you act dignified to a person," she explained to her slightly dazed-looking mother, "then the person acts dignified back. There's a lot more to curtsying than just bobbing up and down, you know."

"Really, Sophie," said Mrs. Hartley. She turned so abruptly into their street that the car ran up over the curb and thumped down again. "You say the most incredible things," she said. "Sometimes I think there's more going on in that brain of yours than meets the eye."

"That's what Dr. Holt thinks, too," said Sophie. "Except all she says is 'Ha!'"

Chapter Nine

"I have a present for you," Dr. Holt said when Sophie came around the corner into the backyard.

"A *present?*" said Sophie. She stopped. This was even more shocking than strawberry short-cake. "For me?"

"Don't get your hopes up," Dr. Holt said. "It's not much."

But Sophie couldn't help getting her hopes up; her hopes were always up when it came to presents. She loved everything to do with them. The wrapping paper. The bows. The feeling inside when someone handed her a present that maybe, just maybe, it was going to be the one thing she wanted more than anything in the world.

Half the time, she didn't even know what that one thing was. It was the not knowing that was so exciting.

Dr. Holt waved her hand at a small square package on the glass-top table. "Go on," she said gruffly. "Open it."

It felt awfully light. It didn't really look like a present, either; it was wrapped in plain brown paper. There wasn't a card or anything.

But still. Sophie started to unwrap it carefully.

"I would have thought you were the type to rip right into it," Dr. Holt said as Sophie slowly unstuck the first piece of tape so as not to tear the paper.

"My mother likes to reuse the wrapping paper," said Sophie. This paper had already been used, she could tell. The name of the local grocery store was written in red on the inside.

"If you take much longer with that thing, you're going to have to throw it away," Dr. Holt growled.

"Throw it away?" It didn't surprise Sophie at all that Dr. Holt had strict rules about opening presents. She quickly tore off the paper, tape and all, and opened the top of the box.

It was filled with worms.

"Oh, *thank* you," Sophie said. She didn't stop to think that hugging Dr. Holt might be like hugging a statue with bones. She just hugged her. And even though Dr. Holt seemed a little startled, her return hug was surprisingly human.

"How did you find them?" Sophie asked.

"My daughter helped me," Dr. Holt said gruffly. "You don't think I touched those things, do you? Half of them had crawled away by the time we got out here. She had to dig up some new ones. It was hard work, let me tell you. I ought to make you split your profits with me."

"But they're a present," Sophie said, clutching the box to her chest.

"I know, I know. . . ." Dr. Holt leaned forward in her chair. "How much are you going to charge your father for them?" she asked.

"Seven cents a worm," Sophie said promptly.

"Highway robbery," said Dr. Holt.

She had put the worms in her father's bait bucket in the garage. Now she needed to go inside and figure out how much he owed her. As she came across the yard toward the back door, Sophie saw John and Thad sitting on the back steps. John was the picture of doom, with his elbows on his knees, his chin resting on his hands, and a heavy scowl on his small face.

"I wouldn't go in there if I were you," Thad told her.

"Why?" said Sophie. "What happened?"

"Nora didn't get the part."

Sophie stopped dead in her tracks. "She didn't?"

"Nope."

"I'm going in the army," said John. He banged the heel of his boot against the stairs.

"Who got it?" Sophie asked Thad. "Lauren?"

"How should I know?"

"If girls cry in the army, they kick 'em out," said John.

"Nora's *crying?*" The bones in Sophie's legs seemed to turn to jelly and she sank down onto the step next to Thad.

"She was when she got out of the car," reported John.

"She was when I went into the kitchen," said Thad. "Believe me, you don't want to go in there."

Nora crying. It was worse than Sophie thought. "How does she look?" she said.

"Bad," said John.

"Pretty lame," said Thad.

"She's got boogers running out of her nose," said John.

"John, that's not nice," said Sophie.

"Yeah, come on, John." Thad punched him playfully on the arm. "That's not nice."

"It's what *you* said," protested John, punching him back.

"You boys are mean," said Sophie.

"Hey, little brother." Thad rubbed his arm where John had punched it. "You're getting a bit of muscle there. Let me see."

John sat up straight and held his arm out

like a weight lifter in a magazine. Thad squeezed the tiny lump that appeared and whistled. "Way to go," he said admiringly.

"Thad, what else?" Sophie said impatiently. "Stop making muscles for a minute, John."

"What more do you want?" said Thad. "Nora's crying, Mom's up in her bedroom trying to calm her down. . . ."

"And I've got a muscle," said John. He punched Thad again.

"Come on, Hot Stuff." Thad jumped off the stairs and grabbed the neck of John's T-shirt to drag him along. "Let's go see what you can do with the weights in the garage."

"Don't you even *care?*" Sophie shouted as John followed Thad across the yard, rolling up onto the balls of his feet to make himself as tall as possible. "Nora's crying!"

"What do you expect?" yelled Thad. "Girls are wimps!"

"And boys are cool!" shouted John.

Sophie stayed on the back steps as they disappeared into the garage. Nora was behind her, and those two dopes were in front of her.

Sophie thought the safest thing to do was sit tight, in the middle, by herself.

"We are not turning this into a national tragedy," Mrs. Hartley said firmly to the living room at large as she came in carrying Maura. "Nora got a perfectly good part, and we've all had to worry with her long enough."

"I wasn't worried," said Thad, without looking up from his comic book.

"Me, neither," said John.

Sophie knew he would have said anything Thad said. Ever since their workout in the garage, John had been following Thad around like a puppy.

"Well, the rest of us were, and we've had enough." This was from Mr. Hartley, who had just come home. He kicked off his shoes and dropped slowly into his armchair with a groan. "Can anyone get a drink for a tired man?"

"Thaddeus, go and get your father a soda," said Mrs. Hartley. She put Maura down on the rug next to Sophie and settled herself on the couch with the newspaper. Mr. Hartley turned on the television. Thad and John flopped down on the floor at his feet when they came back with his drink, and they all watched the news.

Sophie pulled Maura into her lap to stop her from crawling all over the picture she was drawing of a queen and ruining it. She hadn't seen Nora yet. Even before her mother warned her that it might not be a good idea to go up to her room right now, Sophie had decided to stay downstairs. As curious as she was to see what Nora looked like when she cried, she wasn't in a rush to actually watch Nora *do* it. The very idea made her nervous.

At first, she felt a bit nervous even waiting for Nora to come down, but everyone else was carrying on so normally, she finally relaxed. Maura kept trying to grab her colored pencils, so Sophie gave her one of her own and a piece of paper, too. She was drawing away happily when she suddenly heard faint footsteps in the hall, and turned to see Nora slip quietly into the room and perch on the arm of the couch. Sophie looked around to see if anyone else had noticed, but no one had. Nora didn't look at her, but sat staring straight ahead. Then Mr. Hartley raised his arms above his head in a great stretch and moved his head around in a slow circle to work his tired neck muscles the way he always did at the end of the day, and saw her. He immediately turned off the TV.

"Let's hear a round of applause for Nora Hartley, Chief Chickadee!" he said in a loud voice like an announcer. When he started clapping enthusiastically, everyone else did, too. Even Maura.

"Oh, Dad, we're not chickadees, we're mourning doves," Nora protested, but she was laughing. Sophie was very relieved to see that Nora's eyes had only the slightest bit of red around the rim. And that the red on her cheeks was from blushing. "And I'm not the chief. I just get to do more of the dancing than the other three," said Nora.

"You'll be wearing a wreath of feathers and a beautiful gray-and-white costume, won't you?" said her father.

Sophie thought gray and white sounded

dull. If it were her, she would have wanted to be a cardinal, and wear bright red. But Nora only blushed and said, "It really *is* beautiful."

"Mourning dove . . . chickadee . . . you'll always be the chief to me," her father said grandly. He held out his arms. "Come give me a hug and no more tears, that's a girl."

Nora didn't even seem to mind that he was treating her as if she were a little kid. She jumped up and looked happy to be enveloped in his huge hug. She hugged her mother, too, but when she turned toward Thad and John, they both cried, "Who-o-o-oa!" at the top of their lungs and scrambled away from her as fast as they could on their bottoms, which made everybody laugh.

Next Nora looked at Sophie. "I'm sorry I've been such a rat," she said quickly.

"That's okay," Sophie said. "I'm sorry you didn't get the part."

"You'll never guess who did."

"Lauren?"

"No. A girl named Hilary. They brought her

in from another school." Nora smiled a mean smile. "She's younger than Lauren, too."

Nora wasn't being kind, but Sophie couldn't help feeling a rush of satisfaction on her behalf. "Serves her right," she said.

Nora pulled something out from behind a pillow in the corner of the couch and held it out. "This is for you," she said.

It was a tiara. A real tiara.

Sophie was transfixed. "For me?" she said.

"It was in the box of old props," said Nora. "They used it in a production last Christmas. Mrs. Ogilvy said I could have it."

Still, Sophie didn't move. She couldn't believe it was a tiara. Or that Nora was giving it to *her*.

"But why me?" she said.

Nora shoved it at her. "For heaven's sake, put it on," she said with a touch of her old impatience. "You've wanted it long enough."

"How did you know?" Sophie said, taking it from Nora and staring at it wonderingly. She felt as if she were in a trance. To think that Nora was giving her a tiara; that her own sister had been able to see deep into her heart and read what was there. It was almost more amazing than the tiara itself.

"The pictures in your drawer, you idiot," Nora said. "How do you think?"

Sophie blinked. "You looked in my drawer?"

"Of course I did. You looked in mine, didn't you?"

"And mine," said Thad.

"And mine," said John. "I put a hair across it."

"Oh, Sophie," said Mrs. Hartley. "I'm not even going to *ask* if you looked in mine."

"If we kept our drawers as messy as you keep yours, we'd be in big trouble," Sophie said indignantly.

That made them all laugh again. Even Mrs. Hartley.

"Go ahead, put it on, Sophie," Mr. Hartley told her. "Let's see how you look."

She felt a little self-conscious, but very pleased, as she went and stood in front of the TV so they could all see her. She stood very straight and put her shoulders back and pulled in her stomach just the tiniest bit. After all her curtsy practicing, she found she felt taller and a little more dignified like that. Then she lowered the tiara ceremoniously onto her head and looked to see in their faces how it fit.

It must have fit perfectly, because they all applauded and smiled.

"Princess Sophie Hartley," her father said. "What did I tell you?"

"Queen Sophie Hartley, please," Sophie said, to which Mr. Hartley replied, "Excuse me, Your Highness," and bowed.

That meant Sophie had to curtsy, so she did. It was a slow and graceful curtsy, with just the tiniest dip of her head at the end. She knew it was one of her best.

She would have liked it if everyone kept clapping for a while longer, but everyone else wanted to get in on the act. Nora jumped in front of her and executed a graceful demi-plié and then did several quick leaps in the air. It sounded to Sophie as if everyone applauded even louder for Nora than they had for her. Then John yelled, "Oh, yeah? Well, watch this!"

and executed a series of karate kicks at the television screen while shouting, "Hi-yah! Hi-yah!" until Mrs. Hartley made him sit down. At which point, Thad stood up, crooked one leg in the air in front of him, and held his arms out to the sides so that he looked like a heron, the way he did when he was preparing for a flying kick in soccer. With the muscles in his long legs standing out and the very still way he was able to stand there, it looked very impressive.

It was one of those times when Sophie was glad to be part of a large family, even if it meant she didn't get to be the center of attention for very long. If her mother hadn't finally told them all to settle down, someone would have probably ended up crying. Someone always did. It might have been Sophie, too, if it weren't for her tiara. She reached up and felt it carefully, pushing it more firmly onto her head. She couldn't imagine how anyone could cry when they were wearing a tiara. Unless it was from happiness, like Miss America.

Sophie blinked a few times to see whether she could raise any happy tears, but she couldn't. No one was watching her anymore, anyway, so what was the point? Mr. Hartley had turned the TV back on so they could watch the sports news.

"Good heavens," said Mrs. Hartley, looking at her watch. "I haven't even started dinner."

"What're we having?" said Thad.

"It's too late to make anything new," his mother said, knitting her brow. "I suppose there's always that leftover liver. . . ."

"Liver?" They all moaned, even Mr. Hartley. There were a lot of gagging noises and clutching of necks and stomachs from Thad and John, who rolled around on the floor for a bit. Then the phone rang, and Nora ran to get it.

"Liver isn't much of a celebration dinner, is it?" said Sophie, and Thad said, "It's an even worse consolation dinner."

"You're right," said Mrs. Hartley. "Somehow, liver doesn't fit the festive mood here tonight. Sophie, run and get the phone book, that's a good girl. We'll order pizza. Delivered."

That got the loudest applause of the entire evening. They were all yelling out orders when

Nora came back into the room and said, "Sophie, it's for you."

"For me?" said Sophie. It was never for her. "Who is it?"

"Some girl," Nora said.

"Hurry up so we can order," said Thad.

Sophie got up—carefully, so her tiara wouldn't fall off—and went into the hall. "Hello?" she said cautiously into the phone.

"It's Heather," said Heather.

"Oh." Sophie's heart sank. "Hi, Heather."

"Next week is my birthday, so my mother said I can invite a friend to go out to a restaurant and a movie and then spend the night on Friday," Heather announced. "Then we're going to go horseback riding the next morning because I used to take lessons in California and I haven't been once since we moved here. I know how to jump."

"Great," said Sophie. She reached up and put a firm hand on her tiara as if she could already feel the relentless up-and-down of the horse beneath her.

"The trouble is," Heather was saying, "I can

only invite one friend. And you and Destiny are tied."

"That's okay," Sophie said quickly. "I don't—"

"So I've decided to hold a contest to see which one of you will get to go," said Heather. "Whoever gives me the surprise I like most at school tomorrow wins."

"What kind of surprise?"

"It has to be something of your own that you really like," said Heather. "That way, it will mean more. But nothing green or pink. Just something you know I'll like. Destiny said she knew exactly what to bring."

Heather proceeded to give Sophie a list of possible presents. By the time Sophie put down the phone, she was looking very thoughtful. She wasn't about to give Heather something of her own. Heather didn't deserve it.

Sophie walked slowly back into the living room as Thad was saying, "You don't know you're talking about. Pepperoni and pineapple is awesome."

"Sophie doesn't want pineapple, either,"

Nora said, looking at her. "Do you, Sophie?"

Sophie actually liked pepperoni and pineapple, but she knew she had to side with Nora. "No," she said to Thad. Then she looked at her mother. "I want liver."

"You *do*?" said Mrs. Hartley.

"I love liver," said Sophie.

Her mother came over and put her hand on Sophie's forehead. "Are you *sure* you're the real Sophie Hartley?" she said, looking into Sophie's eyes.

"*Queen* Sophie Hartley," corrected Sophie.

Sophie crumpled up the piece of paper with her old lists on it and shoved it under her blanket. From now on, she was only going to have one list. She was sick of having two; they kept battling each other in length. Besides, there was no point in adding "Curtsy" to the list of things she was good at when she only had to take off "Being kind." What she was planning on doing to Heather at school tomorrow definitely wasn't kind. But it wasn't unkind, either. There were times when it was more important to stand up for yourself than to be kind, she had decided. And this was one of them.

She pushed the crumpled list down to the end of her bed with her foot as far as it would go. Now that she knew how sneaky everyone in her family was, this was going to be her new hiding place. It was her job to change her bed once a week when her mother put clean sheets in her room, but since all Sophie did was put the clean sheets back in the linen closet and sleep on the old ones, no one would ever know.

She took out a new piece of paper and wrote "Things I Want" at the top and then "Ermine cloak" underneath. She remembered that one thing wasn't a list and chewed on the end of her pencil for a bit while she tried very hard to come up with something else.

She didn't have to put "Tiara" anymore. And she was feeling very satisfied about her "Dignity." There was no point in putting "Throne," either. It would never fit into her room. But what else did a queen need?

Then it came to her: Commoners.

What good was being a queen if there weren't a lot of commoners around to curtsy to her?

As she wrote, Sophie made a vow to herself that she would be very kind to her commoners when she got them so they wouldn't feel so, well, common. She was about to push the new list under the blankets when she stopped. If she hid a list of things she wanted, no one would ever see it. And if no one ever saw it, she'd never get the things she wanted. It would be far better to make a few copies and leave them around the house, she decided. Then maybe someone in the family would buy them for her.

Sophie knew exactly where to start. The bottom of her mother's grocery list.

Chapter Ten

Heather was looking very pleased with herself as Sophie walked slowly up the sidewalk toward her the next morning. Heather was waiting for her at the front door of the school. Destiny was standing next to her. She looked pleased with herself, too. It made Sophie a little nervous the way they immediately put their heads together and talked the second they spotted her. But she held her head higher and kept walking.

"Look what Destiny gave me," Heather said triumphantly as Sophie came up to them. She stuck out her arm. "Two dangle bracelets.

Now I have five." She shook her wrist back and forth in front of Sophie's face in case Sophie hadn't seen them.

Destiny was staring at Sophie with a funny expression on her face. "Is that real?" she said suspiciously.

Heather stopped admiring her bracelets and looked at Sophie, too. "Is that my present?" she asked.

"No." Sophie held out a brown paper bag. "This is."

"It had better be good," Heather said, snatching it rudely out of Sophie's hands. "If it's not," she said threateningly as she opened it and peered inside, "that means Destiny . . . *Eeeuuuw!*" Heather tossed the bag back to Sophie and pinched her nostrils shut. "What *is* it?" she cried. Destiny jumped back as if the bag harbored something alive.

"Liver," Sophie told Heather. "I had it for dinner last night."

Actually, she'd had pizza. She had only put the tiniest piece of leftover liver in her mouth before getting into the car this morning, and she had put a bigger piece in the bag. Some of the liver was still stuck in her teeth. She could hardly wait to get rid of Heather and spit it out.

"I love liver, Heather," Sophie said, leaning forward so she could breathe in Heather's face. "I thought you might like it, too, if you tried it. Liver is very good for you and it doesn't have a face."

"That's it! You lose three points!" Heather's voice was furious, but it was high and funny, too, because she was still pinching her nose. "I hope you're proud of yourself! You made it to the bottom of my list! Come on, Destiny."

She turned and flounced away. Destiny was right behind her.

Sophie was spitting the last remnants of liver into the trash when Jenna and Alice came running up to her.

"What did you do to Heather?" demanded Jenna.

"Where'd you get the tiara?" said Alice.

"I gave her a present," Sophie said to Jenna. "Nora gave it to me," she said to Alice.

Alice and Jenna looked at each other and then at Sophie again.

"Are you still friends with her?" asked Alice.

"Are you going to wear that in Mrs. Hackle's class?" said Jenna.

"No. Yes," answered Sophie.

Alice and Jenna exchanged another look.

"Mrs. Hackle will make you take it off," Jenna said. "You know how strict she is."

"I'll put it back on at lunch," Sophie said. The bell rang, and the three girls turned and headed toward the front door.

"Are those real diamonds?" Alice asked.

"What do you think, Alice?" Jenna scoffed. "Sophie can't afford real diamonds. Can you, Sophie?"

Sophie only smiled.

"They *could* be real, Jenna," Alice said. "You don't know everything."

"Do you want to spend the night at my house tomorrow?" Jenna said to Sophie. "Alice is coming."

Sophie stopped and looked at her. "You were mean to me," she said severely. She turned to Alice. "You were mean to me, too."

At first, it made Sophie feel good to see the guilty way Jenna and Alice looked at each other and then down at the ground. But almost immediately, it made her feel terrible. She didn't want to make them feel bad. They were her friends.

Alice looked up at her quickly and flashed a tiny smile. "I'm sorry," she said.

"Me, too," Jenna said grudgingly.

"I forgive you," said Sophie.

"Can I try that on?" Alice asked, looking longingly at Sophie's tiara.

"Me, too?" said Jenna.

"Maybe," said Sophie. "But you'll have to start out as commoners until you learn how to curtsy."

"Do *you* know how?" they asked together.

"Of course." Sophie had never felt more regal than she did when Jenna's and Alice's mouths dropped open in unison as they watched her.

Only when she was standing upright again did they close.

"Come, commoners," she said kindly.

Then, with shoulders back and stomach in, dignified, kind Queen Sophie Hartley sailed into school with her loyal commoners by her side and her diamond tiara sparkling in the sun, the way it was going to do all day, every day, starting now.